What the critics are saying...

5 Hearts. "DANCE OF THE SEVEN VEILS is not only incredibly, sinfully erotic, but it features two characters that all readers will feel a strong connection to." ~ *Sarah W., The Romance Studio*

5 Angels. "Lyssa's struggle to overcome the low self-image she has from her loveless marriage was handled wonderfully. Savidge was a true alpha male, handsome, rich, and considerate, not to mention so sexy that I wanted to keep him for myself." ~ *Trang, Fallen Angel Reviews*

"What a wonderful debut for the talented Cris Anson. The storyline was well written and the characters captivating. Not to mention the sex was hot! DANCE OF THE SEVEN VEILS is a must buy and I heartily give it 5 unicorns." ~ *Stacey, Enchanted in Romance*

4 ½ Stars. "....a wonderful story of a woman who finds her way after being damaged emotionally by her ex-husband...With passionate encounters so hot the pages start to smoke, this is one story you do not want to miss." ~ *Elise Lynn, eCataRomance Reviews*

4 ½ Stars. "DANCE OF THE SEVEN VEILS is an intriguing exploration of a woman rediscovering her sensuality and her power as a female." ~ *MB, Romance Junkies*

"Anson delivers an erotic and triumphant tale of a woman's struggle with self-esteem. This first book is a spicy and promising start for the DANCE series." ~ *Susan Mitchell, Romantic Times BOOKclub*

"If you like light-hearted romance, with enough steam to fog your glasses, this is a must- read! The humor that flows between the characters, and the human emotions that fill the pages, from lust to laughter to love — this is something that can satisfy you for a long time." ~ *Marissa, Novel Romance Reviews*

"The sex between these two is hot enough to burn up the sheets, but contains an equal amount of emotion making the story more about romance and passion than simply sex." ~ *Sinclair Reid, RomRev Today*

"Lyssa and Savidge are interesting characters whose chemistry radiates from the pages of this book. (Anson) writes like a veteran of the genre and I can't wait to read more of this exciting series from an author who is sure to be a star of erotic romance." ~ *Miaka Chase, Just Erotic Romance Reviews*

Cris Anson

Dance of the Seven Veils

ELLORA'S CAVE
ROMANTICA PUBLISHING

An Ellora's Cave Romantica Publication

www.ellorascave.com

Dance: Dance of the Seven Veils

ISBN #1419952293
ALL RIGHTS RESERVED.
Dance: Dance of the Seven Veils Copyright© 2005 Cris Anson
Edited by: Sue-Ellen Gower
Cover art by: Syneca

Electronic book Publication: January, 2005
Trade paperback Publication: July, 2005

Warning:

The following material contains graphic sexual content meant for mature readers. *Dance of the Seven Veils* has been rated *E-rotic* by a minimum of three independent reviewers.

Ellora's Cave Publishing offers three levels of Romantica™ reading entertainment: S (S-ensuous), E (E-rotic), and X (X-treme).

S-*ensuous* love scenes are explicit and leave nothing to the imagination.

E-*rotic* love scenes are explicit, leave nothing to the imagination, and are high in volume per the overall word count. In addition, some E-rated titles might contain fantasy material that some readers find objectionable, such as bondage, submission, same sex encounters, forced seductions, etc. E-rated titles are the most graphic titles we carry; it is common, for instance, for an author to use words such as "fucking", "cock", "pussy", etc., within their work of literature.

X-*treme* titles differ from E-rated titles only in plot premise and storyline execution. Unlike E-rated titles, stories designated with the letter X tend to contain controversial subject matter not for the faint of heart.

Dance of the Seven Veils
Dance

Chapter One

"...and remember, if you see a naked man handcuffed to the ring in the ceiling, it's because he wants to be there."

Lyssa Markham stumbled in her silver high-heeled sandals as she followed her best friend up the broad steps leading to the portico. Even in pricey Main-Line Devon, PA, this mansion stood out, a sprawling, three-story brick affair with Palladian windows and a wraparound porch, hidden from the street by a tall hedge of slow-growing English boxwood.

"Wait, I'm not sure I want to—"

"Oh, no you don't," Kat Donaldson said. "You're not chickening out now. Uh-uh, no way." She took a firm grip on Lyssa's upper arm underneath the billowing black cloak. "You're making a statement, just remember that. You're thumbing your nose at that scummy ex of yours and you're going to be the belle of the ball."

Taking a deep breath, Lyssa let her hand brush against her face to be sure her white silk half-mask was in place. Between it and the white veil covering the lower half of her face, she hoped no one could recognize her. She could do this. She *wanted* to do this. She wanted to prove she wasn't the frigid, overweight floor-mop that George had divorced. *You don't have to participate,* Kat had said. *If you say "no," they'll leave you alone. That's an ironclad rule. If you only want to look, that's okay.*

Now Kat murmured, "Just keep saying to yourself, 'I'm celebrating the one-year anniversary of my divorce. I'll ogle the men all I want, and if I feel like touching them, I will. And if it feels good, I'll let them touch me back.' You'll do fine, Lyssa. You're a beautiful woman who's unfolding out of a cocoon into a spectacular butterfly. You'll have them buzzing around you like honeybees in a field of clover."

Lyssa's mouth tilted up in a tentative smile. "Aren't you mixing metaphors here?"

"Yes, and aren't you procrastinating? More guests are coming in behind us."

A glance behind her told Lyssa that two cars, a Jaguar and a Mercedes, had pulled up to where two parking valets waited to whisk the cars to the rear of the property when the guests alit. As did Lyssa and Kat, the newcomers all wore half-masks and long black capes, hiding their costumes from prying eyes outside the mansion's five acres of manicured lawn and garden. The masks and capes, Kat had explained, were their "ticket" into the party. There would be no gatecrashers.

"Okay," Lyssa said softly. "Let's go."

She reached out, but before her slightly trembling fingers touched the brass knocker, the solid oak door swung open and a tuxedo-clad giant bowed them inside. *Bouncer*, was Lyssa's first thought. It somehow eased her mind. All the members of this club had been rigorously screened, Kat promised, for physical, financial, and emotional health. Guests had to be approved in advance by a screening committee. Lyssa hadn't even known Kat belonged to such an exclusive club until she'd been invited to tonight's soiree. But, she supposed, with Kat's fine arts gallery situated on upscale Lancaster Avenue in nearby

Bryn Mawr, she came in contact with many wealthy clients and browsers.

A never-married free spirit with a long string of lovers, Kat turned heads with her flippant attitude, flamboyant auburn hair, whiskey-colored eyes and funky wardrobe. Lyssa herself leaned toward the look of understated elegance she'd grown up watching her mother wear.

Not that any of it mattered tonight, Lyssa thought wryly. Her own scanty costume, that Kat had autocratically said she would supply, couldn't be worn on the streets of downtown Philadelphia.

The giant relieved them of their black capes and gestured to a room beyond an exquisitely carved archway reminiscent of a Roman aqueduct. Taking slow, almost reluctant steps, Lyssa allowed her eyes to roam the spacious foyer. A Bokhara rug in soft reds covered a portion of the checkered black-and-white marble floor. Atop the rug stood a beautifully carved library table, decorated with an alabaster vase filled with dozens of fresh, fragrant calla lilies. A chandelier the size of a beach ball, lit with hundreds of sparkling crystal lights, hung from a ceiling that, Lyssa gauged, was probably fourteen feet high. Along one wall, a sweeping staircase wide enough to handle hoop-skirted Scarlett O'Haras led to the second floor, where bedrooms no doubt awaited some. *Don't go there*, her mind warned.

The drawing room beyond the archway was softly lit by wall sconces and dozens of candles clustered on the massive marble mantel, imparting a rosy hue to everyone's skin. The veils of her costume swirled sensuously around her, stroking her bare legs, as Lyssa slipped into the room. She was conscious of the slight swaying of her unfettered breasts beneath the nearly translucent silk. Kat had already disappeared into the darker recesses of the room. She was on her own.

A good-looking, bare-chested young man wearing tight black pants and carrying a silver tray of champagne flutes stopped, dipping his tray in invitation. She took one, hoping the glass would act as a kind of barrier-cum-moral support and hoping the contents would settle her nerves. As she sipped, she edged into one of the shadowy spaces between the sconces. The room seemed to be at least forty feet long, divided into seating areas on one side — long, pillowy sofas, she noted — and an open space where, in the dimness, she perceived several slowly moving shadows that she presumed were dancing partners.

On one of the sofas, she noticed a man settling down on his back. He wore only a loincloth and bear-tooth necklace. Red ochre stripes decorated the exposed part of his face. Another Indian, this one in full feathered headdress and a long, shapeless leather smock laced up from neckline to hips, pulled the reclining man's arms over his head, tied his wrists with rawhide strips, then fastened them to a table leg.

As Lyssa watched, transfixed, the Indian chief began unlacing the smock, then slid it slowly off his — no, she realized — *her* shoulders and down to her feet. Unabashedly naked, with a feather tattoo on the outer curve of her right breast, she pulled one, then two feathers from her headdress and began to stroke the bound brave's skin. Slowly up, down, up, down his tanned body, from neck to ankles and back again, until Lyssa could see him grit his teeth in a grimace of arousal that could not be assuaged. The squaw leaned forward, large breasts hovering tantalizingly above his face. A distinctive lump lifted the loincloth, growing larger with each languid stroke of the feathers.

Lyssa gulped her champagne. She could feel her breath coming more heavily. What would it be like to be so totally dominated by someone arousing you, teasing you, being captive but knowing that you wouldn't be hurt, someone bringing you to the brink but not knowing when release would come?

She shivered deliciously and turned away.

And bumped into a red-haired, red-bearded man wearing nothing but a kilt. The wiry hair on his wide chest brushed against her bare arms and she shivered again. *That must be how the feathers felt*, she thought, surprising herself. She looked up into the shadowy depths of his eyes behind the mask, deep blue like a loch on a clear day. And saw unmistakable desire flare through them.

"Ah, lassie, may I touch you?" he asked with a hint of a Scottish burr.

"You can," she breathed. *Where had that quick acquiescence come from? He's a stranger!*

Slowly he raised his hands to her shoulders and with a butterfly touch stroked her arms down to her wrists, then back up again. The sensations rocking through Lyssa astounded her. Here she was, in a roomful of strangers, allowing a nearly naked stranger to fondle her, and she didn't want to move!

The Scotsman took the edge of one of her veils and dragged it slowly sideways, the soft, translucent silk abrading her nipples with its movement. She could feel them pebbling, tightening into hard peaks. A tremor ran through her.

Apparently taking that as encouragement, he lowered his head to her shoulder, and his lips followed the line his fingers had made down then back up her arms. His bushy beard contrasted with the delicacy of his mouth. Lyssa closed her eyes and gave herself up to the sensation. She felt his mouth move to her collarbone, dropping moist, nibbling kisses that tickled and nipped, while his hands stroked her cheeks, her neck, then, soft as a whisper, to her breasts.

Tensing, Lyssa opened her eyes. As if attuned to every nuance of her body, the Scotsman raised his head in silent question. Lyssa worried her bottom lip with her teeth, uncertain how to extricate herself. The feelings he evoked in her quite contradicted George's brutal assessment of her that she had been an unfeeling blob in bed during his quick, mostly unsatisfying sexual encounters. Yet here was a stranger who was fondling her in full view of a score of others. And she was responding.

"Ah, lassie," he crooned, "yer a dream come true, with yer green eyes and blonde hair, with the body of a goddess and the reactions of a satyr. If you decide you want a taste o' Scotland, I'll be here all night waitin' for ye."

He took one of her hands in his, lifted it to his mouth then turned it over to give her palm a slow, licking kiss. He closed her fingers around the kiss and, with a rueful sigh, moved on.

For one long moment Lyssa stood immobile, stunned by his casual comment. A stranger had seen more passion in her than her ex had! Had she really been as frigid as he'd always complained?

Well, this was the perfect opportunity to find out, she decided. Had Kat hoped this would happen? That she would discover her own sexuality? After all, she'd married George at eighteen and gotten pregnant right away, and he'd been her only lover.

She eased her way around a curly-haired woman bent forward over an oak sideboard, her short leather skirt riding up over hips that showed no sign of panties, being spanked with the flat of a devil's hand. In a far corner she saw what Kat had mentioned earlier, a man handcuffed to a huge ring anchored in an exposed ceiling beam. He was naked and it seemed to Lyssa that he was being totally ignored. She wondered if he enjoyed bondage and punishment, for his eyes behind a black mask seemed to avidly take in the action around him. Judging by his boner, he was receiving plenty of vicarious pleasure.

After snagging another flute of champagne to ease her dry throat and hopefully slow her racing pulse, Lyssa wandered to the other side of the room, her face and figure briefly spotlighted as she passed the lighted candles on the mantel. When she reached the dance area, she could hear soft music, something operatic without words, from *La Traviata*, she thought, something to heat the blood and invite slow, sensuous movement, preferably close to another's body.

She found herself swaying to the rhythmic music as she watched a couple in identical long black robes—a witch and warlock?—moving more or less as if they were having sex standing up. The music came to an end and they separated briefly, giving Lyssa a glimpse of two bare bodies underneath their open robes. Her skin heated. She could feel a flush creep from her ears to her cheeks, her neck, down to her breasts. The man's glistening, upright penis told her they had in fact been doing exactly what Lyssa had imagined.

Another piece of music issued from hidden speakers, this one a bluesy jazz sound with a soulful saxophone in a slow, sexy tempo that had Lyssa wanting to hold someone and dance as close to him as she could. She felt the flute being removed from her hand as a fireman in a long yellow slicker came up to her. He was just slightly taller than she, so that their eyes, and lips, were almost on a level. His dark eyes glowed fiercely as he gazed on her mouth that had softened from watching the previous couple. He leaned forward slightly and flicked his tongue across her mouth under her diaphanous veil. She felt the delicious shock of it down to the center of her sex. With a soft sigh, she unconsciously inched toward him, needing to feel more. It had been too long since a man had kissed her, and the sensory bombardment she'd already received this evening had aroused her more than she could have imagined just yesterday.

He pulled both sides of the slicker apart and hauled her up against his naked length. One hand came around her shoulder; the other took hold of her hand as in a normal dancing stance. He slid the hand down from her shoulder to the small of her back, tightening his hold. With the other he positioned her palm on his hairy thigh. And started swaying to Coltrane and the blues, snuggling his erect penis against her. "I've always dreamed of holding Marilyn Monroe in my arms," he murmured into her ear. "And now I've got her. All soft curves. All woman."

For a moment Lyssa went shell-shocked at his comment, then relaxed a bit and reveled in the warmth, the safety of being wrapped in strong, male arms. She relished the feel of his hard cock pressing between her legs, evidence that she was a desirable woman. Heat from his swarthy skin radiated through the thin silk into every pore, raising her internal temperature almost to a point where she had to reciprocate.

Suddenly she felt heat on her back as well. Someone—unmistakably a man, naked as well—pressed against her from behind. Large, callused hands settled around her waist. She felt the slight scrape of five o'clock shadow against her nape, warm breath in her ear. He, too, seemed decidedly aroused, his engorged penis finding the cleft between her buttocks and moving his hips suggestively.

A shiver that was half panic, half desire, zapped through Lyssa. Eyes closed, she allowed herself to live in the moment, to examine her dichotomous reaction to what Kat had once laughingly called a "man sandwich" with her as the filling. In the prim, repressed part of her mind that George had boarded up tight, she knew she shouldn't be allowing this, that she was merely a handy receptacle for two indiscriminate males in heat. Yet, in the part that was awakening to adventure, she knew that nothing would happen without her consent, that Kat had somehow known she wasn't frigid but only needed an opportunity to discover that fact, that she had had some part in arousing these two sexually sophisticated men who took more and more intimate liberties the longer she stood quiescent.

She could feel the two penises, hard, hot, urgently seeking, which had somehow snuck under her veils and stroked her, skin against skin, skin against pubic hair. Their breathing became more ragged, and hers along with it, their hands touching, caressing, stroking her in every place they could reach.

"No." It came out a whisper. She opened her eyes, cleared her throat. "No," she said, more forcefully.

She knew she was blushing furiously. She couldn't meet the fireman's eyes as he slowly, regretfully, took a step back. The other did as well, his hands slow to leave her waist, trailing his fingers as if trying to prolong contact. Would they think she was merely a cockteaser? *So what? She'd never see them again.*

One didn't just jump into something like this, she rationalized. Why, even with salsa she started out mild, only gradually building up her palate to the point where she enjoyed the sizzling chilies. To herself she could admit that the feelings she had experienced in the past several hours had exceeded anything she'd known in her life. But to give these two strangers access to her orifices because she had allowed them to arouse her — she just couldn't.

"Sorry," she said, head bent down in something akin to guilt. It was the George syndrome all over again, an inability to satisfy a man, freezing up at an inopportune moment, her congenital inadequacy surfacing with a vengeance.

"Sweetheart," the man behind her murmured, "you've nothing to be sorry for. You're the hottest firecracker I've ever lit. If the other guys knew the feel of you against them, how shivery you react, they'd be lining up for a chance to touch you."

He brushed his lips against her nape in a parting gesture. "And I'm sure as hell not going to tell them. I want to be first in line."

And he was gone.

In her peripheral vision, Lyssa noted the fireman, incongruously barefoot with his slicker, still stood near her. She lifted her head, thrust out her chin, ready to flinch at a stinging putdown she was sure would come.

"I second the motion." He smiled, a slow, sensuous smile full of hunger, and turned to snag a longneck bottle of beer from a passing waiter's tray. "To you," he said, lifting the bottle in tribute. "The new Marilyn Monroe. Sex goddess incarnate."

And he moved into the shadows, leaving Lyssa alone while her heart pounded and her breasts rose and fell with her labored breathing. She could hardly believe it. She, whom George had called a fat cow, had captured the interest of several attractive, virile men. Were they just seeking new blood? Or was Kat right, and she was a desirable woman?

Kat. There she was, in the next room through pocket doors that hadn't been open earlier, a candlelit room decked out with buffet tables. Kat's riotous auburn hair—a wig, Lyssa realized—cascaded down below her hips, strategically covering portions of her torso, with her slender legs and feet bare. Lyssa's breath stopped. *She didn't!* But it looked like Kat was costumed as Lady Godiva.

Lyssa came to Kat, whose face and skin were flushed with a sheen of perspiration...and a glow. Lyssa refused to speculate on whether Kat had availed herself of one of the bedrooms. After all, the purpose of this party was to, well, mingle. Wasn't it?

"You look different," Kat said thoughtfully. "Like a hungry cat that had a taste of cream and wants more."

"Oh, Kat, I never dreamed I could..." She worried her bottom lip again.

"Could get so hot and bothered?"

Lyssa felt her face heating under the mask. Darn, she wished she didn't blush so easily. "You were right. It's so…liberating…to know that it wasn't me. I felt…delicious. Desirable. Sexy beyond belief. One of them even compared me to Marilyn Monroe."

"You are all that, my friend, and more. You're like Sleeping Beauty waking up from a long, poisoned-apple sleep. And you're going to find a Prince Charming who will appreciate what you have to offer."

Lyssa made a sound in her throat, half skepticism and half longing.

"Seriously. When we first came here, I ducked into the shadows so I could watch. You should have seen some of the reactions. Every man's head turned. Some of them reached for their cocks just so they could dream it was you touching them."

"Oh, stop it, you're just making that up."

"It's true. You don't know just how lovely you are. You have a soft look about you, like you're ready and waiting for Him. With a capital H. Like you could make love all night."

"Oh, no, I'm not ready for that. I think it'll take me a long time to really…give myself to someone wholeheartedly." She twisted a strand of her blonde hair around her finger. "But I think maybe, some time in the future, it's possible. I never knew I could feel so…"

The noise level in the drawing room had risen. They turned to see, then wandered back through the pocket doors. In a spotlight, a belly dancer was gyrating her hips to Saint-Saens' *"Bacchanal"* from *Samson et Delilah*, focusing her efforts on a man dressed like a pasha right down to his turban, who sat alone on one of the sofas. As the music became more animated, so did her movements. She unhooked her jeweled bra and tossed it on his lap, then divested herself of one gauzy bloomer leg, then the other, and finally her girdle and panties. The music ended with her wearing only a jewel in her navel, and she flung herself onto the sofa amid applause, straddling the pasha, as the spotlight faded.

"Wow," Lyssa breathed. "That was soooo sexy. What moves she has!"

"Any woman could make those moves if she has the right audience. They've been married about a dozen years. They say this adds spice to their love life, and he's so proud of the way she looks, the way she dances." Kat chuckled. "The way she turns other guys on."

Kat elbowed Lyssa, inclined her head to the archway leading to the foyer. "Like him. That gladiator. I'd like to be the one to turn *him* on."

Lyssa's heart skipped a beat, then thudded back to catch up. About six feet tall, dark hair curling around his ears and nape, a narrow black mask that accented the sharp cheekbones and square jaw, the gladiator leaned negligently against the jamb, arms crossed, one leg casually crossed over the other. A gold medallion glowed against a thatch of dark chest hair overlaying well-sculpted muscles. Sandals were laced up his calves, and his thighs under the short Roman tunic looked strong enough to hold him over her in a variety of positions for hours.

She blinked. *Where had that thought come from?*

The gladiator inclined his head slightly, raised an eyebrow. In invitation?

Lyssa swallowed hard. Her heartbeat accelerated. She realized she *wanted* to go to him. But her feet felt rooted to the parquet floor. Lingering doubts about her femininity choked her.

In the background the music shifted. The frenetic opening strains of Richard Strauss' *"Dance of the Seven Veils"* wafted through the hidden speakers, tympani pounding, a haunting oboe solo connecting to her synapses. Her heart stuttered. It was as though fate had stepped in at this singular moment in time, sending her gaze to this particular stranger across this crowded room, the music reminding her of her costume of seven diaphanous veils tenuously held in place by a golden waist chain. In her eyes, the gladiator morphed into the lascivious, depraved Herod that the voluptuous Salome would entice into granting her deepest, darkest wish.

The gladiator moved languidly to a pile of plush cushions on the floor of a dimly lit alcove and reclined on his side, one knee upraised, leaning on an elbow. He swept his other arm out in a gesture of "The stage is yours" and waited, his mouth curled upward into a slight smile of anticipation.

You're Salome, a voice said inside Lyssa's head. *Amoral, decadent, willful. Dance for him. Seduce him.*

She thrust out her chin and posed like a dancer, the toes of one foot pointed out, one arm across her torso. She scribed a graceful arc up and over her head, then down to one hip, allowing her fingers to skim lightly up her thigh and between her breasts, as if calling his attention to the charms within the circle, ending with a graceful *salaam* gesture at face level.

Taking a deep, fortifying breath, she grabbed the edge of one veil, removed it from around her waist and dropped it to the floor at his feet. The sensuous music slowed to the *leitmotif* that was Salome's signature, infusing her blood with fire. She locked gazes with him — with Herod — and tugged another veil free. Raising it high, she allowed it to float down over her hair, then dragged it down peekaboo fashion until her eyes showed, then her nose, her lips. He transferred his intent gaze to her pouting mouth, and licked his lower lip. Lyssa felt a shock of pure lust course through her. She wanted him to kiss her. Everywhere.

The music shifted to a faster tempo, compelling her to rotate her hips, to bend and sway to the music. Her hair sifted over her face in a golden curtain. She gripped the third veil and trailed it over her breast until the sensitive peak tightened and tingled, then flung the veil aside.

Faster still, the music urged Salome to tempt King Herod to his limits, to hypnotize him, to make him *want* to grant her most perverse wish. Another veil slipped from her body, baring both her breasts. She bent toward him, teasing him, offering her hard, pink nipples to his view but just out of reach. She spun around, undulating her arms and shoulders with her back to him, then removed the veil that covered her ass cheeks. The languid Salome *leitmotif* recurred, relentlessly ratcheting up the tension. She rolled her hips in a slow front-to-back motion, imitating the sex act, as she turned slowly, slowly to face him.

The lust in Herod's eyes, the pupils so dilated they looked black, almost brought Salome to her knees. Absently she noted that his tunic tented up almost to his upraised knee. And *she* had done this to him. King though he may be, Salome knew she had spun a carnal web of obsession around him.

Frenzied now, the exotic music rushed to its climax as Salome divested herself of the penultimate veil across one restlessly moving hip, flinging it into the alcove, where it landed on Herod's muscular shoulder and slid down unnoticed. The last long obbligato sounded, the oboe trill drawing out the tension to an almost unbearable level. Salome ripped off the veil covering her golden thatch and stood before her King, triumphant, panting, exquisitely naked but for the waist chain and golden sandals, the veil in her raised fist fluttering with her harsh, hot breaths.

The music ended with a turbulent cadenza punctuated by three furious chords. Salome fell to her knees and collapsed, legs on Herod's lap, arms flung above her head, her naked skin sheened with perspiration, thighs spread apart without thought to modesty, open to her King's lustful gaze.

Panting, Salome slowly became aware of the flickering candlelight, of the muscular legs of King Herod under hers. Through lowered lashes she could see her flushed breasts rise and fall with every deep breath, the pink nipples standing erect, the areolas puckered and tight. Became aware that every nerve ending cried out for his mouth, his hands, his cock. Anywhere, everywhere, just satisfy this...this *craving*, this need for release that she'd never experienced before.

He shifted her so she lay on her back and he beside her, his leg slung over her thighs, his hard cock pressed against her hip. Bending forward, he captured a nipple in his mouth and suckled. No tender touches, no coy foreplay, his mouth felt as though he was starving and she was nectar for the gods. Her back arched upward violently, offering herself to his greed. Her hands swung down to grab his head and keep him anchored there, feasting on her breast, her nipple, her very soul, willing him, no, *demanding* that he relieve the relentless itch in her other breast.

When he did, she groaned in relief and pleasure. Carnal need spiraled higher and higher within her, infusing every nerve ending with electric current. The heat of his cock against her hip made her twist her body so that it would touch her where she burned the hottest, between her thighs. She wanted him to bury that fiery sword inside her, wanted him to pound his body into hers, fuck her until she ached, and then fuck her some more, until she melted into a puddle of warm honey in his arms.

From somewhere far away, she heard a deep chuckle, felt the vibrations from his chest to hers. "Not yet, temptress," he whispered into her ear.

"Yes," she hissed, squirming to get closer to the thick, hot cock that was driving her crazy.

Ignoring her demand, he inched his way down her torso, licking, nibbling, suckling on bits of her skin. He paused a moment to dip a hot tongue into her navel. She twitched, pressed his head down into her belly, wanting more. Her crotch burned for him. She wanted to feel his weight pushing her deep into the cushions, wanted to feel the rasp of his chest hair rubbing against her aching breasts. She wanted to wrap her legs around his hips, crush him to her as he pounded into her. Her breath came in great, wrenching gasps, the oxygen in her lungs having been consumed by this fire inside her that burned hotter and hotter with every stroke of his tongue.

She writhed under him. Needed him. *Now!*

"Please," she begged, almost incoherent with passion.

In response, he edged her thighs farther apart and settled himself between them. His large hands crept up her inner thighs, leaving behind trails of fire. She felt his thumbs settle on the lips of her slit and gently tug them apart. She thrashed on the cushions, flinging her head from side to side, lifted her hips up to him, moaning, pleading, begging for…something, anything to relieve this volcano building inside her.

She felt soft puffs of air on her most private parts, and gasped. Her face flamed. She'd heard of this, but had never…

"Oh!" He touched her with his tongue. The sensation was unlike anything she'd ever experienced, like brushing against a live electric wire that sent a high-voltage current to every part of her body. She felt his tongue take long, slow laps up her slit, felt moisture gushing from her. She closed her eyes in embarrassment.

"You taste so good," he murmured from between her legs.

Then she felt his hands grip the undersides of her spread knees and lift her legs, planting them squarely on his shoulders, lifting her butt clear off the floor and exposing her slit to his unobstructed view. She could feel the heat creep down from her face and up from her slit, so that she envisioned herself as one large, blushing rose petal.

She didn't have time to dwell on it. Because he fastened his mouth on her lower lips and suckled deeply.

She almost jumped out of her skin.

Her fists clutched handfuls of his hair. Without her conscious direction, her hips began bucking. *More.* She wanted more, more of his mouth, more of him.

She could feel his tongue probing deep within her. She was too enthralled, too drugged to be embarrassed now. Something inside her was building, building, ready to explode. Her world narrowed to one spot on her body, the nub of her sexuality that he seemed to be avoiding, even though his mouth, his tongue, avidly touched and suckled every other part nearby.

"Please," she begged again, moving her hips even while she inched his head up to the spot by pulling on his thick hair.

Another deep chuckle reverberated through him into her bones. He raised his head, looked directly at her. Their eyes met. She felt as though, with that look, he touched into the very soul of her, the hidden part no one had ever discovered, and knew in some visceral way that she would never be the same.

Then finally, finally, thank you God, his tongue landed on her clit. He laved it, then suckled, then gently took it between his teeth and pulled.

She slapped her palms flat on the cushion to lever herself harder into his mouth. All her tension, all her heat, came together in one massive explosion that rocked her hips higher off the floor. She made some deep, guttural moan that sounded as primitive as she felt, as though the world had just coalesced from rudimentary atoms to become a heavenly body of one man and one woman linked together in the most elementary, mind-blowing fashion that was the primary reason for existence.

From somewhere outside herself, she felt him gently lower her legs to the cushions and draw himself up to her. She felt his tender kisses on her closed eyes, her nose, her temple as aftershocks kept pulsing through her now-boneless body. He kissed her facial veil and kissed her gently on the mouth and she tasted herself on him, a combination of musk and heat and his brandy.

He pulled her into a fierce embrace. Slowly she became aware of the feel of his chest hair rubbing against her breasts, his hair-roughed thigh scraping her legs, the cold medallion around his neck between them. Felt his hot cock against her hip, undiminished while she was totally sated. Heard the harsh rasp of his breathing.

Heard something else. Murmurs. Words.

Applause.

Applause? Oh God, where was she?

It came to her like a strobe light. She was Salome, lying on a cushion, with King Herod half draped over her, ready to grant her most perverse wish, his hard-on about to burst against her.

Another strobe flash—candles burning in alcoves. Voices. Faces coalescing out of the shadows.

Not Salome. The haze slowly lifted and Lyssa returned to herself.

The gladiator.

Dear God, what had she done?

Reality returned with the rude awakening of a dip in the ocean on New Year's Eve.

She had just allowed a man, a total stranger, to go down on her in front of a roomful of people, had not only encouraged him but had enjoyed a mind-blowing orgasm the likes of which she'd never realized she was capable, and was reclining like an odalisque in a painting, naked as the day she was born, smelling of heat and sweat and sex and unable to curb the cat-in-cream smile on her face.

"Salome…" he began.

"No!" Disentangling herself from his arms and legs, Lyssa struggled to sit up. She glanced around wildly.

Amused faces stared back at her, avidly drinking in the drama in the alcove. Couples, singles, pairs of women draped in each other's arms, groups, all of them in various states of undress, if not outright nakedness.

The masquerade. *Orgy*, she mentally corrected herself. And she'd been a willing participant. *Oh God, she'd die of embarrassment!* She spied the archway through which she'd first entered and shot to her feet. With a deep breath that didn't quite calm her, she thrust her chin out and dared anyone to stop her as she marched, head held high, to the foyer to retrieve the sheltering cloak the bouncer had deposited in the closet.

Chapter Two

She finally realized what the painting needed. Eyes. Hidden eyes, gazing at the mirage that wasn't a mirage.

Lyssa stepped back from the easel and cocked her head as she studied the almost-finished painting, a cross between Rousseau's primitive jungle style and Maxfield Parrish's swirling, sinuous lines. In the foreground a black panther, a leopard, and several other sleek, predatory animals dipped their heads down, pink tongues darting out to drink from a shimmering waterhole that she fancied resembled a reclining nude in abstract. Surrounding them, lush foliage grew in profusion—greens, yellows, browns of all hues.

A drop of perspiration trickled down Lyssa's forehead. Absently she swiped it away with the back of her hand, then dipped her sable-tipped brush into a daub of burnt umber.

"Right there," she murmured, applying strokes with abandon at the opening between two large acanthus leaves.

"Now the brows."

"Do you always talk to yourself when you paint?"

Lyssa jumped, dropping the brush. Her hand went to her heart. "Good grief, Kat, you scared me! Why didn't you ring the bell?"

"I did." Kat's wry tone matched the slight upward curve of her lips. "Three times. That's when I decided you must be out back in the studio. So I just let myself in through the French door."

"Oh. When I'm in the middle of a painting, I kind of lose myself."

"Yeah. You look like you haven't eaten or slept since Saturday afternoon."

"Thanks a lot, *friend*." Her smile softened the implied criticism in the tone of her voice. Still, she removed the scrunchie, ran her fingers through her blonde hair, and refitted the elastic band snugly on the ponytail. Bending down to retrieve the brush, she cleaned it with a turpentine-soaked cloth, then set both on the table near the easel.

Kat moved to the wicker chair in the uncurtained bay window flooded by late-morning light and sat down, her gauzy broomstick skirt swirling around her ankles. She looked elegant as usual, Lyssa thought, mentally comparing her own paint-spattered smock and thong slides to Kat's cool, put-together look.

"What are you painting?"

Lyssa knew Kat was itching to see what she was creating, but tactfully waited for an invitation. With good reason. The first time Kat had come around the easel before the painting was ready for viewing, she had laid down the law. *No one will put a hex on my creativity by sneaking a peek.* Not even her best friend.

She was tempted to let the other woman stew. She still hadn't totally forgiven Kat for talking her into going to the masquerade party two nights ago.

Party. Hah! It was an orgy, pure and simple.

She felt her cheeks heat. And she, Lyssa, had jumped in with both feet. And legs and arms and torso. All totally naked. And glorying in it!

"So. What did you think of your gladiator?"

Darn it, Kat knew her too well. She'd obviously seen the blush that natural blondes couldn't hide and assumed, correctly, where her thoughts had strayed.

"He's not *my* gladiator," she said in a furious hiss.

"But you'd like him to be, hmm?"

Lyssa stepped around the easel and removed her smock, carefully hung it on a hook on the wall. The lazy breeze from the ceiling fan felt good on her bare arms. She uncapped a bottle of Evian and took a long swallow, then carefully recapped it.

"Okay, lady, stop stalling and sit down. As Joan Rivers would say, 'Can we talk?'"

It was hard to meet her friend's gaze as Lyssa sat in the adjoining chair, the wicker squeaking softly. "I can't believe I did what I did."

"You followed a natural inclination. That idiot you married had you so hoodwinked you thought you weren't any sexier than a ten-pound sack of sprouting potatoes. But believe me, you made a terrific impression on everyone."

Lyssa's blush heightened. Sure. As wanton as she'd acted, she was certain she made an impression. But what *kind* of impression still needed to be ascertained. What if someone who'd attended *knew* her? What would she say to him or her if they mentioned it?

"Seriously, Lyss, wouldn't you like to see him again?"

"No! I couldn't."

"Too bad. He'd love to meet you formally. He did ask about you, you know."

For a moment Lyssa was taken aback. But, she realized, if Kat was a member of this so-called club, she would know other members. She'd probably even talked to him about... She stifled a groan. "I don't think I could look him in the eye."

Suddenly restless, Lyssa jumped up. She didn't want to think of it. Looking him in the eye, having him leer at her, knowing what he knew of her, how quickly she popped off as soon as a stranger's tongue touched...

Damn! "Would you like to see what I'm working on?"

"You bet." Kat's eyes sparkled as she darted to the easel. Lyssa couldn't help but think that Kat saw right through the charade, that she'd rather have someone see a closely guarded work-in-progress than to talk about a naked gladiator who'd probably had dozens of women throw themselves at him, herself included.

The silence lengthened as Kat studied the three-by-two-foot canvas. It was a larger format than she usually worked, but her muse had demanded it. She held her breath, waiting for Kat's pronouncement.

"This will be the centerpiece," Kat declared at last.

"What are you talking about?"

"You absolutely have to have a one-woman show."

"We've been through this before. I'm just dabbling here, Kat. Nowhere near ready for the public. I don't even have that many pieces. After George left, I only picked up my brushes again to fill an empty spot in my heart."

Kat turned to her with narrowed eyes. "I've been in the art business for ten years, three of them in my own shop. I've sold millions of dollars worth of paintings. I have a pretty good feel for what the art-buying public wants. And you, Lyssa Abigail Markham, will be the next darling of the art world. Believe me, people will want to buy your work."

She looked back at the painting. "Especially this one." There was a peculiar tone to her voice that Lyssa couldn't decipher. "We'll mark it 'Not For Sale'. That will make you all the more desirable."

"I don't think—"

Kat rode right over Lyssa's objection. "The conception and execution are brilliant. On first glance, it looks like an ordinary bunch of wild animals drinking at a waterhole. It took some looking, but I can see the hidden figure. First you just see sunlight bouncing off the shimmering ripples created by the tongues of those animals lapping up the water." She gestured to the area under discussion. "But then...oh, my..."

Her voice trailed off. She swallowed. Then her pitch kicked up a notch. "That's your blonde hair trailing through the water. These animals aren't drinking. They're *licking* the figure. *Arousing* her. Arousing *you*." Kat's smile grew. "Just like your gladiator," she finished triumphantly.

"No, no, that's not at all what I had envisioned..."

"It's what I see on the canvas," Kat declared with a decisive nod.

Lyssa worried her lower lip. Had she created an erotic Rorschach inkblot? Had she let her uninhibited reaction to the gladiator color what she'd poured into this painting? She'd thought it so subtle that no one else would notice the subtext. It had been like a compulsion, to put on canvas what she'd seen in her mind's eye. She hadn't done it by conscious design. Like a conjurer's trick, it had appeared on the canvas when she had stopped after a frenzied day of painting yesterday and looked, really *looked*, at what she'd done. And this morning, she realized what it needed to complete the vision — the several pairs of eyes watching the seduction.

It was the orgy, she knew. Her unconscious mind trying to assimilate what she'd done.

Was her mind absolving her of her lingering guilt over her quick capitulation to the gladiator's expert stroking? Or was it mocking her, announcing her blatant sexual foray to the world?

Her uncomfortable musing was interrupted when the front doorbell chimed its three-note announcement.

"I thought you couldn't hear the doorbell from here," Kat said.

Lyssa smiled. "You can if you're not wrapped up in another world." She ran damp palms over the sides of her loose-fitting yellow slacks as she made her way down the front-to-back hall of the house her ex had been so happy to leave.

"Sign here, please," a man in a FedEx uniform said when she opened the door.

With a frown, Lyssa took the clipboard. She couldn't imagine who would be sending her an overnight package on a Monday morning. "Who's it from?"

The man shrugged.

She scrawled her signature, still mildly annoyed that she had kept her married name because of her college-bound daughter, and exchanged the clipboard for the packet.

Good grief, her daughter. If Michelle ever heard what she'd done... But Lyssa knew that she wouldn't have gone with Kat if Michelle hadn't been at her about-to-be-roommate's home for the weekend.

That reminded her. She'd best make sure her newest creation was inside the studio's closet before Michelle came back today to do some last-minute packing. Lyssa hadn't been happy her daughter had chosen to spend her last weekend before college away from home, but at eighteen she was almost an adult, and Lyssa didn't have the heart to forbid her to go.

She glanced at the dahlia-painted wall clock as she came into the well-equipped kitchen, where Kat was rummaging through the fridge. "Wow, it's after twelve already. Want to stay for lunch?"

"I'd like to," Kat said, opening a bottle of Evian, "but I have to get back to the shop and relieve Sandy."

"Too bad. I have some leftover lasagna I was going to nuke." Lyssa pulled the strip that opened the cardboard FedEx package and slid out a business-size envelope.

"Rats. Anything you cook is worth eating, even leftovers. Who's it from?"

A tremor skittered down Lyssa's back under a V-neck top screen-printed with big sunflowers. "George's lawyer." She reached into a drawer and pulled out a steak knife, idly wishing she had the nerve to stick it in George's neck. Or his philandering appendage. One year divorced and he still had the power to irritate her. Opening the envelope, she scanned the letter.

"That lousy, rotten...ooooh, when I get my hands on him..." Furious, she slapped the letter onto the granite countertop. "He can't *do* that! It's in the divorce decree!"

"What'd he do?"

With an angry grunt, Lyssa picked the letter up again. "Oh, it's couched in legalese, but I can just hear the smug voice of that sleazy lawyer putting the idea in his head. Listen to this. 'Because of the recent and continuing plunge in the stock market, the current dividends from Mr. Markham's portfolio are insufficient to meet his obligations regarding his daughter's tuition. Inasmuch as his assets are fairly illiquid, we require a window of three months beyond the due date to judiciously dispose of enough assets to cover this obligation.'"

She grabbed the kitchen phone and speed-dialed. "When I get hold of him, he'll be eating his balls for supper."

Impatient, Lyssa paced the tile floor while waiting for someone to pick up. Then muttered, "Naturally, I get his answering machine." She waited a moment, then controlling the violent urge to swear at him, took a calming breath and said, "George, it's Lyssa. This is very important. Please pick up if you're listening. Something's come up regarding Michelle, something urgent. Can you call me as soon..."

She stopped as she heard someone pick up.

"Hello, George?"

"You're the ex-wife, aren't you?" the female voice said.

"Yes, this is Lyssa Markham. Is George there?"

"Oh, no. He took MariBeth on a cruise."

Lyssa closed her eyes and willed her blood pressure not to explode. "Can he be reached?"

Gum snapped in Lyssa's ear. "You're kidding, right?"

Another deep breath. *Calm down.* "May I ask who this is?"

"I'm MariBeth's sister. I'm cat-sitting for the week."

Lyssa rested her forehead against the refrigerator door. She didn't believe it. He didn't have the money to pay their daughter's tuition but could find some spare change to take his bimbo on a cruise, for God's sake! And cat-sitting? She almost found the energy to smile. The image of an allergic George trying to share his new home with a cat was the only bright spot in this whole mess.

"Do you have his itinerary? What's the name of the ship? Or at least the cruise line? When will he be back?"

"Saturday. I don't know where they were going, or on what ship or whatever."

"If you hear from him, please, I beg you, have him call me. It's about his daughter. There's something he's got to know urgently. Will you do that, please?"

"Yeah, sure. Does he know your number?" More gum snapping.

"He should, but please take it down in case he didn't take it with him." George had better remember his daughter's number, but if he'd been bedazzled enough to gift his scrawny little plaything with a cruise, he might not even remember the number of his stateroom. She recited the number and, with another plea to have him call, Lyssa hung up.

"Bad news, huh?"

"I don't believe it! A cruise! And that gum-popping teenybopper who answered the phone doesn't even know the name of the ship! What if there'd been a real, life-or-death emergency? It would serve him right if his house was robbed while he was—"

"Hey, Lyss, calm down." Kat thrust a glass of iced tea in her hand. Lyssa gratefully took it and drank half of it without stopping.

Calmer now, she said, "He knew darn well he had this expense coming up. This should have been paid weeks ago and they're just telling me now? Where am I going to get fourteen grand overnight? He knows how tight my budget is, what with taking over the mortgage payments. He's deliberately putting Michelle's freshman year into jeopardy just to spite me."

She picked up a sponge from the kitchen counter and rubbed vigorously at a spot on the faucet. "Three months. That's practically the whole first semester. Dartmouth will never let her matriculate without payment in full, especially not freshmen."

She briefly closed her eyes and took a deep breath. "Illiquid assets, baloney. If he hadn't bought that mansion for that bimbo, *MariBeth*," she spat the name like an epithet, "he'd have enough liquid assets."

"Can you call your lawyer and ask if he can legally do this?"

Lyssa stared through the patio door at the mature pin oak in the backyard, weighing her options. She barely noticed the lush green leaves rustling in a slight breeze, or the ripe tomatoes hanging on their sturdy stems in the garden.

"Or better yet," Kat added, "go to that sleazy lawyer of his and demand some action."

"You're right. I have to do *some*thing." Still, she stood indecisive for a moment. Then she spun on her heel, her slides squeaking on the Mexican tile floor. "I'd better get cleaned up."

"Atta girl. Don't take 'no' for an answer."

Her daughter meant the world to Lyssa. She wasn't going to settle for anything less than a fourteen-thousand-dollar check from that shyster. One that wouldn't bounce. Or George was going to be in big trouble.

* * * * *

She couldn't be more than nineteen, Lyssa thought as she nodded to acknowledge the pretty receptionist's invitation to have a seat. Shining black hair so straight it might have been ironed, a heavy dose of mascara around her brown eyes, a very snug beige knitted sheath. She had surely been chosen to make a statement—This law firm is for the beautiful people.

Lyssa glanced around the richly appointed reception room as she waited for the executive assistant to escort her to George's attorney. Cordovan leather wing chairs, large photos of the Philadelphia skyline, fresh flowers, sleek computer and phone system, all announced that Quick, Bowers & Savidge was one of the most prestigious law firms in Philadelphia. George must have paid Jack Bowers a fortune, judging from the surroundings.

Who was she kidding? He'd have had to, the way the settlement was structured. She hadn't wanted to "take him to the cleaner's", as Kat had suggested. She just wanted to be rid of him. The last ten years of their nineteen-year marriage had been loveless, and he'd become emotionally abusive. Perhaps she should have allowed her own lawyer to be more forceful and not settle for a too-large house with a too-large mortgage, refusing alimony but accepting child support until Michelle graduated from college. She'd thought his agreement to pay for her college expenses had been set in stone.

She should have known better than to trust a lawyer.

"I'm sorry, Mrs. Markham, but Mr. Bowers is in court. May I help you?"

Lyssa turned toward the rich alto voice. The woman looked her own age, with chestnut hair cut in a sleek, shoulder-length style and artfully applied makeup. Her black Donna Karan suit fitted her tall, slender curves like Saran wrap on a bowl. It made Lyssa wish she'd worn her own power suit, but she'd had to use Michelle's eight-year-old Acura with the nonfunctioning air conditioner. Her own Honda CR-V was packed chock-full with college-bound stuff, which she fervently hoped would be on its way to New Hampshire in two days. She'd settled for a silky A-line dress in butter yellow and bare legs in high-heeled sandals.

She tamped down her urge to snap at the woman. It wasn't her fault her boss was in court. Unless it was just a stalling tactic.

"When will he be back? It's rather important."

"Actually, the case is scheduled to run for the remainder of the week. May I inquire the nature of your visit?"

Lyssa glanced at the receptionist, who was looking up something on her computer for a caller. She didn't want the entire office to know her ex was creating a problem. Apparently reading her mind, the assistant gestured Lyssa into a conference room off a short hall whose floor boasted an Oriental runner the rich shade of rubies.

"Thank you." She nodded to acknowledge the assistant's thoughtfulness. "I really need to talk to someone about your client's nonperformance of his contract."

"And the client would be...?"

Were they *taught* to be obtuse? "My ex-husband, George Markham. I received a FedEx letter today from your boss."

"Oh, I'm sorry. I should have been more clear. I'm Robert Savidge's assistant. He's Mr. Bowers' partner. If we knew the nature of your concern, perhaps Mr. Savidge could help. He happens to be in the office this afternoon. I'm sure he can spare a few minutes to straighten this out."

"Thank you. Please tell him your company's client is reneging on a clause in the divorce settlement that couldn't come at a more inopportune time. My daughter is leaving for Dartmouth in two days—she's a freshman. We were just informed this morning that George is unable to meet his obligation. Which means she won't be able to matriculate."

"I see. Why don't you have a seat here. Let me locate Mr. Markham's file and see if there's something Mr. Savidge can do."

Lyssa murmured another thank you and marveled at the way the woman seemed to glide out the door. She oozed a sensuousness—as opposed to the receptionist's blatant sensuality—that was all the more seductive because it seemed unconscious.

"What are you, an idiot?" she muttered. "You're in enemy territory. Don't start empathizing with them." Still, she wondered if all the women in the law firm were chosen more for their looks than for their ability.

The conference room, the size of a small dining room, sported a round cherry table and four armchairs padded in forest green paisley. Lyssa studied excellently executed prints of leaf silhouettes in myriad shades of green on the walls. Idly she wondered if the law firm was one of Kat's clients.

"This way, please, Mrs. Markham."

The assistant led her down the hall and into an open area with a well-appointed workstation, then knocked on an ajar door. "Go right in."

"Thank you," Lyssa said yet again. Taking a deep breath, she nudged the door with her palm. It opened onto a spacious room dominated by a massive walnut desk. On one corner she noted two wooden file trays holding stacks of papers. An opened file lay on a blood-red leather blotter. Behind the desk, a long credenza held a computer whose screen-saver showed a sailboat slowly gliding through calm waters. The high-backed, well-padded executive chair was empty.

As she took a few nervous steps into the room, Lyssa felt her high-heeled sandals sink into an Oriental rug, its blues and reds and creams glowing with the soft patina of age. Behind her she heard the door close with a solid click, the well-trained admin giving the client privacy with her attorney. It was a corner office, she noted, unadorned windows revealing a clear view of the venerable City Hall, with its verdigris statue of William Penn jutting into the hazy blue of the sky. Against the brightness of one window near the corner she saw the silhouette of a tall man with broad shoulders, apparently mesmerized by the skyline. Hesitantly, she approached. Still he didn't turn.

"Excuse me," she finally said.

She had to skirt a seating arrangement of leather club chairs in order to get close enough to snag his attention. "Mr. Savidge?"

He turned then, the window light revealing the sharp planes and angles of a face that could have graced a Roman temple. Long, thin blade of a nose, dark hair curling around his ears, eyebrows arched like a raven's wings, lips as sultry and ripe as a *GQ* model's. Lyssa's heart stuttered. He looked like...

The corners of his mouth turned up. A smile lit his night-dark eyes.

"Lift up your skirt."

"Wh-what?" *It couldn't be!*

He took two steps toward her, like a panther stalking a gazelle. "I said, lift up your skirt...Salome."

Lyssa felt her cheeks heat like molten lava. *The gladiator!*

"You-you're Robert Savidge?"

He made a sweeping bow. "At your service." He took another step forward. Although totally intimidated by his approach, she was rooted to the spot. She couldn't tear her gaze away from his mouth, the mouth that knew her so intimately...

"And you do know what kind of service I provide, do you not?" His voice, a low, sexy hum, vibrated through her very bones.

"You're even more beautiful without a mask," he murmured, lifting his right hand to stroke her cheek with a knuckle. "I wonder how you taste."

His thumb caressed her lower lip. Involuntarily, she licked the spot he had touched and a shiver coursed through her. She thought she heard him groan, but it could have been her imagination. He bent his head and flicked his tongue over the spot hers had just dampened.

Her knees threatened to buckle. Her gladiator was doing it again, robbing her of sanity, bringing her to instant lust like Pavlov's dog salivating at the ring of a bell. She grabbed him by his biceps to stabilize herself. Strong, flexible muscles under soft, summer-weight wool, she vaguely noted, her gaze trapped at the sight of the full lower lip, the tanned skin making his teeth seem whiter. She lifted her gaze to his eyes.

Mistake. In their dark brown depths she saw a searing desire that made her moist between her legs. How could he do this to her with just a glance, when she'd been unable to please George in even the most basic way?

His face hovered over hers, only inches away, as if awaiting permission — or inviting her to act. She couldn't stand it a moment longer. She followed a sudden whim and licked his jawline, inhaling a subtle fragrance that was part citrus, part fresh air, and part aroused male. Then she lifted up on tiptoe and captured his earlobe with her teeth.

He inhaled a harsh breath then placed his hands on her waist, lifting her high enough to fit his mouth over her breast. With a whimper, she arched her back, clenched fistfuls of his curly hair as she strained to pull his head closer. He suckled and pulled at one breast through the thin silk, then moved to the other, leaving its mate damp, cool, puckered — and wanting more.

As if of their own volition, her legs wrapped themselves around the gladiator's waist. He shifted his arms to her butt cheeks, pressing her closer to what she immediately perceived was a very large erection. In some needy corner of her mind, Lyssa gloried in the fact that she was able to bring him to such a tumescent state in what seemed like only a minute.

But she had no time to ruminate on that fact. She felt him moving, striding across the room, to the massive desk. He placed her on the outer edge, leaned behind her and swept the file folder to the floor, then forced her down until her back rested on the blotter. He pulled her legs from around his waist and lifted them, draping her knees over his shoulders. Her dress slid up to reveal high-cut, lace-trimmed panties. With a groan he pulled the crotch roughly aside, bent his head and licked her slit, sliding his tongue up and down, thrusting it between her engorged lips to taste her essence, then suckling on the nub that contained, it seemed, every nerve ending she possessed.

Suddenly Lyssa found herself bucking her hips into his face. Again. With a last bit of sanity, she remembered there were people outside that door, and bit her lip to keep from crying aloud. She grabbed his hair to hold him between her legs while she felt spasms rock her, felt heat burst from her center down to her toes and up to her hairline. Oh God, he'd made her come in less than five minutes! And she wanted more. Much more. But there was something she'd come here to do.

She languidly tried to see through the lingering haze of sensuality to remember what it was, when she heard a muted click, then a tug, a whisper of sound, and the pressure from the elastic in her panties ceased. In her dazed state, she decided this masterfully Alpha man would be the type to simply cut away an offending garment. Before she could follow that train of thought, she heard the hiss of a zipper, the crinkle of foil.

Then he loomed over her, grabbed her hips with two strong hands. "I've thought of nothing but this since Saturday night," he rasped as he thrust a hard, hot cock into her sheath.

Lyssa stifled a cry as pure lust shot through her. *This* was what she'd come for. She abandoned herself to the sensations exploding within her, the exquisite feel of him plunging and withdrawing, the searing heat radiating between them. He bent over her, pushing her legs up so that her knees touched her shoulders. The movement lifted her hips off the desk, allowing him to sink even deeper inside her. She could swear his cock touched all the way into her womb.

He leaned forward and moved his hands up to grasp her shoulders, holding her in place as he pumped hard, harder and yet harder still into her, savaging her mouth with his. She felt the pressure build within, the delirious climbing to a higher level of ecstasy. Her hands scrabbled for purchase against his clothing, wanting, needing the feel of his skin against her palms. Finally she settled for reaching behind him to grab his firm ass cheeks through the supple wool and bring him even closer. He made one long, low moan, lifted his head and went rigid. Their eyes met.

The connection sent electric explosions through Lyssa. She felt her sheath violently contract around him, squeezing his cock rhythmically as his own spasms rocked them both, until she subsided into a nether world where nothing existed except the scent of him, the heat, the feel of them wrapped around each other.

After a time, she heard him say, "Don't move."

As if she could.

Gradually Lyssa's awareness returned. Legs up in the air, dampness between her thighs, hard desk under her back.

Oh God. She was in Robert Savidge's office, her twat exposed to anyone who might walk in. She tried to lever herself onto her elbows, but her muscles refused to cooperate. She'd been laid, good and proper, unlike anything she'd experienced in her life, and wanted nothing so much as to lie still and savor every delicious memory.

"Here, let me do this."

Lyssa turned her head to see the man she'd just fucked — there was no other word for it. It had been just like Erica Jong's zipless fuck with a stranger. Suit jacket hung impeccably on his broad shoulders, striped tie knotted to perfection, wavy black hair flawlessly combed — God, what hers must look like! — he looked ready for depositions instead of the man who'd given her the most memorable orgasms — orgasms, *plural*, she marveled — she'd ever had.

Then she felt the warmth of a soft, moist cloth cleansing her slit and she fell apart.

"I'm sorry about your panties," he said, touching a dry towel to the area he'd just cleaned. He offered his hands to her and helped her sit up.

Embarrassed to look him in the eye, she quickly stood. Then realized what he'd meant about her panties. The shredded crotch dangled down the back of her thighs. He *had* cut the offending garment! She blushed and averted her head, futilely brushing her palms down the front of her skirt to remove the telltale wrinkles.

He tossed towel and washcloth to the floor behind his desk, then bent down to retrieve the papers he'd scattered when he'd positioned her on the desk.

The papers. *The divorce decree.*

Oh God. He was the enemy. His idea had undoubtedly been to distract her until she forgot she needed a check for fourteen grand to pay for Michelle's tuition. One lawyer watching out for another lawyer's client and never mind who gets hurt along the way.

And he'd done a bang-up job distracting her. How could she have been so bedazzled by the man? How could she have done this with a stranger? Not once, but twice? She couldn't face him, not now, maybe not ever. She had to leave. This minute. She'd call the receptionist from home and insist on having Mr. Bowers call her whenever he returned, no matter how late. She couldn't, could *not*, spend another minute in this man's presence, could not sit down and talk to him rationally and coolly as if they were merely attorney and aggrieved party.

Frantically she glanced around. She'd had a purse when she walked in the door to this lion's den. Ah, there it was, on the sofa. She'd obviously dropped it when he picked her up and snuggled her to his...

No! Don't think it. Don't. Even. Think. It.

She grabbed the purse while his attention was still diverted to the papers on the floor and strode to the door. She wrenched the knob, wondering if his assistant had locked it, a conspiracy between them to muddle her brain into acquiescing to George's machinations.

It opened. Heat flooded her face. What if that woman in the Donna Karan suit had interrupted them while they were—?

Taking a deep breath, squaring her shoulders, Lyssa marched out of the office, her eyes looking neither right nor left, averted her glance from the administrative assistant's work station, marched down the hall past the receptionist, and out through the double glass doors into the elevator lobby. And did not look back.

Chapter Three

Lyssa stood at the butcher-block counter, slicing the chicken breast into slivers while her daughter set the table. As soon as Lyssa had gotten home from the law office, she'd stripped off the yellow dress and tossed it in the laundry hamper, shimmied out of her unsalvageable panties, stuffed them into a plastic baggie and buried them under a week's worth of garbage in the kitchen trash bin. Then she'd taken a long, hot shower, scrubbing the scent of him from her skin. She thanked the gods that she'd been able to get her emotions under control before Michelle had been dropped off by her new roommate after spending the weekend getting to know her and her parents. She'd decided she wouldn't upset Michelle needlessly. She wouldn't tell her about George's crying poverty unless and until it was unavoidable.

Perhaps Mr. Bowers would return her call this evening, especially after Lyssa had impressed upon the receptionist in her phone call how urgent the matter was. Thankfully the young woman hadn't thought to ask why the other partner hadn't been able to help her.

"How much more packing do you have to do?" she asked, pleased that her voice sounded calm and normal.

Michelle shrugged. "Just my makeup and stuff."

"Stuff" had a way of adding three suitcases to the mix, Lyssa knew. "I assume this 'stuff' will fit in the Honda? Last I looked, we'll be lucky to be able to see out the rearview mirror."

"Oh, Mom, this is nothing. Ginger's dad has an Expedition. You should see all the stuff *she*'s taking."

Lyssa poured a dollop of oil into the heated wok. "Are you about ready to eat? I can start stir-frying any time."

Michelle opened the fridge and pulled out the pitcher of iced tea. "Okay. Go to it."

The chicken slivers hit the wok with a sizzle. Lyssa deftly stirred while her daughter poured tea over ice cubes in two tall glasses, then returned the pitcher to the fridge. Lyssa tossed the julienned veggies into the wok. The timer dinged.

"Could you drain the noodles, 'Chelle?"

"Sure."

As Michelle scooted to the other side of the stove, Lyssa smiled to think how well they worked together in the kitchen. She was glad her daughter had absorbed her own love of cooking. Too bad she hadn't learned to clean up the kitchen after herself.

Lyssa was splashing soy sauce into the mix when the front doorbell rang. She jumped. *Jack Bowers*, she thought. Who else could it be at seven-thirty in the evening? Hurriedly she turned off the burner. "The stir fry's ready, honey. You sit down and eat. I'll be right back." She rubbed her damp palms on her apron while she strode down the hall to the front door.

Wondering how she'd explain Mr. Bowers to Michelle and wishing he'd called first, she pulled the door open without looking through the peephole. The breath whooshed out of her.

"*You.*"

He looked even more impossibly handsome in well-tailored khaki trousers and a light blue silk shirt, long sleeves rolled up almost to his elbows, top two buttons undone. Lyssa swallowed hard, resisting the temptation to pat her hair into place, to remove the ruffled apron from around her neck, to wish she hadn't donned comfortable, ratty shorts after her shower. The sudden heat that zapped through her body had nothing to do with the August temperature or the lingering warmth from the stove and everything to do with images of his mouth, his hands, all over her eager and welcoming body.

"Good evening, Mrs. Markham. May I come in?"

"What are you doing here?" she asked, blocking the doorway like a sentry on duty.

Robert Savidge pointed to the attaché case at his feet. "I'm sorry to disturb you at home, but Jack Bowers' paralegal asked me if I could take care of this, since time seems to be of the essence and Jack is tied up in a major trial all week."

He seemed to be acting as though this afternoon hadn't happened. She supposed she should be grateful for his sensitivity, but some small part of her felt disappointed that their primitive coupling had meant so little to him that he could sound so aloof and businesslike.

"Why didn't you call instead of coming here?" It came out a rough whisper. She didn't want Michelle to see this man, to pick up on her weak knees, the lust in her eyes even now, when she knew he'd done what he'd done only to distract her from pursuing their client.

He raised a dark, perfectly arched eyebrow. "Would you have listened to me?"

Lyssa glanced behind her. She hoped Michelle couldn't hear them from the kitchen. "Look, can I call you later? My daughter and I just sat down to dinner—"

"And you don't want her to know there's a problem, right?"

A relieved sigh escaped her. "Yes."

Savidge gave her a long, hard stare that she was hard-pressed to meet, but determined that he blink first. He did.

He reached into his shirt pocket and pulled out a business card. "My home number's on the back. I've read George Markham's file. Call me later tonight. I think I might be able to help you."

"Why should you help me? I'm not your client."

He stared at her long enough for the unspoken message in his eyes to resonate inside her chest. *Because I want to fuck you again.* Then he turned on his heel and strode down the walkway to the Porsche Boxster at the curb.

Lyssa couldn't help herself. She watched the movement of his tight ass underneath the form-fitting khakis as he walked. Then, furious with herself, she spun on her heel and tried to think up a plausible fib to tell Michelle.

* * * * *

"This is Lyssa Markham. You have a solution to my problem?"

She knew she was being abrupt, but the thought of calling Robert Savidge at home, wondering if he was in the same room that she was in right now—the bedroom—could cloud her judgment if she wasn't vigilant. She'd told Michelle it had been one of those religious fanatics at the door, handing out brochures and preaching their faith, then felt guilty all throughout the meal. Luckily, 'Chelle hadn't pursued the matter, and had gone to her room after eating to chat online with her friends.

It wasn't her relationship with Robert Savidge she was hiding, Lyssa argued with herself. She was shielding her daughter from her father's perfidy.

Savidge's voice vibrated low and sexy in her ear. "I have a number of suggestions."

Lyssa gripped the phone harder. His voice poured over her like warm honey over French toast. She wanted nothing so much as to have him lick it off her skin...

"But I think the best one is this."

She realized she had reclined on top of the bedspread, boneless and soft. She sat up abruptly, then took the cordless phone with her to sit on an uncushioned side chair. She would *not* speak to him *in bed*.

"And that is?"

"I see by the file that Quick, Bowers & Savidge is the fiduciary for Miss Markham's trust fund. As the attorney of record, Jack usually signs the checks, but they have to be requested in writing by the trustee."

"And that's George, of course." Lyssa couldn't keep the bitterness from her tone. Of course, it was all his money. She'd married him at eighteen, and had dropped out of college when she became pregnant right away. When George started earning big fees at his brokerage firm, he wouldn't let her work, but doled out small amounts of "throwaway" money that she didn't have to account for. Everything else she paid for by a credit card whose statement he received, or the joint checking account that he reconciled. So he knew what she'd bought and how much she'd spent.

"Yes. Mr. Markham is the sole trustee. Since he obviously asked Jack to write that letter you received today, we can't go that route."

Lyssa bristled. "I *know* that."

Unfazed, he continued. "Here's how we can get around that. Quick, Bowers & Savidge can advance the trust fund a loan of fourteen thousand dollars for three months with interest at prime, with the trust as collateral. Jack can sign the loan agreement as fiduciary, and I can sign the check for the firm."

Lyssa sat up straighter. "Really? It's that simple?"

"We'll have the papers drawn up first thing tomorrow, so Jack can sign before he goes to court. I'll sign the check and you can pick it up at, say, noon." Savidge lowered his voice to a soft purr. "Then I'll take you out to lunch to celebrate."

She could just picture the way he'd suggest they have lunch…pouring champagne on her belly and licking it off, smearing peanut butter on her breasts and —

Good Lord, what was the matter with her? That money had to be in Dartmouth's coffers tomorrow! She tamped down, hard, on her raging libido, tried to ignore the sensual pull of his voice caressing her like a tongue.

"Not a check." Her voice sounded forceful. She was proud of herself. "It has to be wire transferred. I'll call Mr. Bowers' assistant first thing tomorrow morning with the bank routing number. And she can call me back when she gets confirmation of the transaction."

A soft laugh rippled through the phone into her ear, kissing the skin all the way down her throat. "As you wish."

Disappointment speared through her. Obviously he'd only mentioned lunch as an apology for his unconscionable behavior earlier in the day, which he had no desire to repeat.

Dammit, she didn't either! She had no business even *thinking* that way. He was a stranger. She knew nothing about him. Except that he was a successful attorney who wore hand-tailored suits, who had a creative solution to a thorny legal problem, who made love like she'd only dreamed of...

He had hung up.

Lyssa felt bereft.

Chapter Four

"I'm sorry, Mrs. Markham, but you do have to come to the office to sign some documents before the funds can be transferred."

Lyssa bit back a retort at Andrea's pronouncement. Quick, Bowers & Savidge were doing her a favor with this loan. She couldn't blame the admin if there was some unforeseen paperwork to make it legal. If she ran into Savidge, she'd freeze him with a look. "I'll be there in an hour."

Briefly she considered wearing the killer Manolo Blahniks that Kat had insisted she buy along with her other indulgence, a red Jones New York, so she wouldn't look like the poor cousin next to Andrea. But Michelle would want to know where she was going all fancied up. So she settled, almost defiantly, for loose-fitting beige slacks — let him try to do another desk job around *that* bit of apparel — and matching silk shell with low-heeled sandals.

With a blithe, "I've got to run some errands," she bade her daughter farewell and drove to downtown Philadelphia, parking in a garage a block from the lawyers' offices in the prestigious One Liberty Place.

Squaring her shoulders, Lyssa pushed open the double glass doors for the second time in as many days. Recognizing her, the receptionist said, "Just a moment, Mrs. Markham," and picked up the phone to announce her.

Instead of Andrea greeting her, Lyssa heard the low, sexy baritone that had sent shivers down her back before.

"Come right in," said Robert Savidge.

She steeled herself to acknowledge him dispassionately. Her resolve held as she turned to see him without a jacket, the French cuffs on his white shirt held in place with gold and onyx cufflinks, yellow striped tie loosened, top button open. Damn, why did he have to look so sexy, so...approachable?

He led her, not to his office, but to an anteroom adjoining it. Like its neighbor, the room had a marvelous view of the skyline. Lyssa could see the Convention Center sprawled a couple of blocks beyond City Hall. A sofa and two wing chairs surrounded a massive coffee table that held a number of documents. He gestured her to the sofa, but she chose one of the brown-and-gold flame-stitched chairs, ignoring the upward crook of his mouth. He took the other chair.

All business now, he walked her through the documents, including the affidavit she needed to sign. It was just for the record, he'd said, but the law firm needed documentation as to why they had incurred the lien obligation and issued the wire transfer. She signed where indicated; he signed the acknowledgement.

"Let's get the banking wheels in motion," he said, standing with the documents in his hand. "I'll be right back."

She hadn't realized how tense she'd been until Savidge left the room and she relaxed her guard. He'd made everything seem so simple.

At ease now, she gazed around the chamber. Richly paneled with cherry wainscoting, a very healthy potted ficus in a corner, multi-line phone on a cherry side table, everything bespoke low-key elegance. With a wry smile, she contrasted these surroundings with her own divorce lawyer's suite — no-nonsense office furniture, diplomas and certificates on walls, Spartan conference room. And she'd gotten exactly what she'd paid for, she realized. She hadn't wanted to be one of those angry divorcées who stripped their ex of every cent, but, she acknowledged, perhaps she could have been a tad more grasping.

The hallway door opened. "Hi. Mr. Savidge asked me to bring some refreshments."

Lyssa half turned to see the lovely admin coming toward her, carrying a small silver tray with two tall glasses filled with something white and frothy, Sprite maybe, or 7-Up. Andrea walked like a runway model, long strides showing a lot of thigh under the high, off-center slit of her black skirt. Her waist-length red jacket encircled her ribs tightly, emphasizing the curve of her breasts.

Not two feet away from her, the graceful woman tripped. The tray tilted, spilling the contents of both glasses smack on Lyssa's silk shell. Lyssa jumped up with a squeak of dismay.

"Oh, my God, I'm so, so sorry," Andrea gushed, setting the now-empty tray on the coffee table with a clatter. She turned to the side table, pulled out a striped hand towel from the drawer and began to blot and stroke Lyssa's front to absorb the soda.

"It's okay," Lyssa said, trying to take a backward step.

"No, I apologize. I'm wearing a new pair of heels and I'm not used to them yet. This has never happened before." She continued stroking, her motions becoming slower, more deliberate. Lyssa felt her nipples turn to hard little pebbles under the admin's hand.

"The executive washroom's right here. This is silk, isn't it? Gosh, I certainly don't want that beautiful top to stain. Come with me." Andrea grabbed her by the upper arm and tugged her to a door that Lyssa had thought was part of the paneling. It opened to reveal a full bath with walk-in, tiled shower with sliding glass doors, john, and hand-painted sink set into a long, marble-topped vanity.

Once inside, Andrea shut the door with a firm *click*. "Take off your blouse. We have to sponge off the soda right away." She opened a cabinet built into the wall and pulled down an ironing board, then reached inside to retrieve a hair dryer. "Come on, if we hurry, we can get you fixed right as rain before Mr. Savidge comes back with the confirmation number of the deposit. The hair dryer might be enough, but I'm plugging in the iron in case we need it."

Why was she hesitating? Surely she had misconstrued Andrea's languid strokes on her breasts. They'd pebbled of their own accord from the icy liquid splattered across her chest, Lyssa argued with herself, and not because of any desire engendered by a woman's touch. Or maybe it was her lingering thoughts about what Robert Savidge had done to those breasts...

Resolutely she slipped the wet silk over her head and handed it to Andrea, avoiding eye contact.

"The bra, too." Andrea set the garment on the marble counter and stroked the wet silk with a damp sponge. "Won't do any good to put a dry blouse on a wet bra."

With dismay Lyssa saw herself reflected in the mirror covering the entire wall over the basin. The white lace looked transparent. Her nipples stood out, dark pink, erect, and…aching.

"It's not like I haven't seen them before," Andrea said, her attention seemingly on her chore.

"What?"

She looked up then. "Saturday night. You did an excellent Dance of the Seven Veils."

Heat flooded Lyssa's face. She felt the blush creep all the way down, making her breasts an even rosier shade.

"I was the Indian. With the feather tattoo on my right breast?"

Lyssa was afraid to meet the admin's eye. The memory of the boner tenting the loincloth of the Indian bound to the table made her throat dry. Briefly she wondered at the identity of its owner. Then the memory of her own dance that ended with her sprawled naked on the lap of the gladiator — Andrea's boss! — swamped Lyssa. She leaned weakly against the counter.

Andrea set down Lyssa's garment and the sponge. Her fingers went to the buttons of her jacket. In seconds they were undone and she slipped the jacket off her shoulders and let it fall to the floor. Her breasts sprang forth unfettered by a bra. "See?" She lifted her right breast to exhibit the eagle feather tattooed on its outer curve.

Lyssa swallowed. She vividly remembered the shape of those breasts, the teasing sway of them over the trussed Indian, remembered how the Indian lifted his head to capture first one, then the other ripe offering in his mouth, how the woman with the feather headdress arched her back in ecstasy.

As if giving her time to decide, Andrea positioned the silk shell on the ironing board and unconcernedly began to dry it with the hair dryer, her freed breasts swaying slightly with the movement of her arm.

I'm being ridiculous, Lyssa thought. *We're two grown women. We've both seen other unclothed women before.*

Besides, if Andrea had been at the masquerade, if she'd known in advance who Lyssa was—as Robert Savidge had known, according to Kat—then her modesty was misplaced. She probably came across as two-faced, playing the puritan now after having shamelessly allowed a stranger to lick her most intimate places in full view of an avid audience.

The thought of Robert Savidge's tongue on her slit while her hips bucked, of his cock inside her yesterday, the frantic, urgent fucking, the fever-pitch rising like a runaway train that they couldn't—wouldn't—stop, caused Lyssa's breath to come shorter. As if of their own accord, her hands reached up to touch her breasts, to stroke the hard tips into even more unbearable hardness. Her mouth softened, remembering the way he had suckled them while lifting her off her feet before carrying her to his desk. She wanted, needed his mouth on them *right now*.

She pulled the front clasp open and shimmied out of the wet, sugar-sticky bra. In her peripheral vision she could see, reflected in the mirror, two bare-breasted women standing close enough to touch each other if they but lifted their hands. She hadn't heard Andrea turn off the hair dryer, hadn't heard her come up next to her. She simply stood there, breath locked in her throat.

The admin lowered her head and, gently cupping one of Lyssa's breasts, slowly licked the sensitive skin all around the areola. Lyssa's eyes closed as she unconsciously arched into the other woman's mouth. She wanted to grasp the admin's thick chestnut hair and pull her even closer. She wanted her to suck on the nipple, not tease all around it with her knowing tongue.

She couldn't believe she was allowing this to happen. Robert Savidge had turned her life, her values, upside down. A shudder coursed through her as Andrea took as much breast into her mouth as she could fit, then with a delicious suction, pulled backward until it popped out of her mouth. "Mmmm, sticky sweet." She did the same to Lyssa's other breast. "Tastes like Sprite," Andrea murmured. "The real thing. Not diet stuff."

The admin lifted her head, looked into Lyssa's eyes, daring her to reciprocate.

"I—not—no, I can't." She denied her desire, although her chest heaved with arousal. "I'm not ready for…" She couldn't say it.

Andrea's face broke into a soft smile. She placed gentle hands on Lyssa's shoulders and turned her to the mirror running the length of the counter. Several inches taller, Andrea looked down at Lyssa's upthrust breasts from behind her, trapping Lyssa between her hips and the counter. "Look how beautiful you are," she said, her voice a low, silky hum, her fingers skimming down the front of Lyssa's torso, cupping the undersides of her breasts, reaching up to tweak and pinch the nipples. "No wonder he's so taken with you."

Through the continuing sensual haze the admin's touch aroused in her, Lyssa managed to ask, "Who?"

But Andrea simply continued stroking, tweaking, arousing her nipples to even harder, achier peaks. The areolas pebbled roughly, contrasting with the delicate smoothness of the skin surrounding it. Lyssa closed her eyes and savored the streaks of lightning zapping down to her crotch. She wanted Savidge's mouth there, to capture the lightning, to taste her juices.

"May I join you?"

Lyssa's eyes sprang open. As if conjuring him from her dreams, Robert Savidge's face appeared reflected in the mirror. Trapped as she was between Andrea's hips and the counter, Lyssa couldn't move. Two furiously red spots appeared on her cheeks as she watched him unbutton his white shirt and slide it off broad shoulders and let it drop to the floor.

The admin shifted slightly, allowing Savidge's naked chest to press against Lyssa's back, although she kept her hold on Lyssa's breasts. His arms encircled both women at the waist. He nuzzled Lyssa's neck as one hand nudged Andrea's from its hold, replacing it with his own thumb and forefinger. He rubbed and pinched one nipple, plucking, squeezing, tugging, all the while nipping her ear, her neck, whatever part of her jaw he could reach, with his teeth.

Helpless against the onslaught of two experts, Lyssa found herself leaning into him, opening herself up to the two different kinds of strokes, one soft and feminine, one harsher and more masculine. Her breathing became choppier. She felt pressure building against her clitoris as it rubbed against the edge of the cool marble counter.

Suddenly she found herself turned around. Savidge's hands came up to trap her face for a bruising kiss of excruciating intensity. He crushed her bare breasts to his chest. The feel of crisp hair scraping her already unbearably sensitive breasts nearly brought her to a climax.

Lost in that kiss, it took a moment for Lyssa to realize that the side button of her slacks was being manipulated. She heard the sound of her zipper being released, felt the tug of fabric as it—and, oh God, was that her panties, too?—skimmed down her hips and fell to the floor. But both of Savidge's hands still cradled her face as his tongue plundered inside her mouth.

Andrea. Andrea was aiding and abetting her boss.

This thought sent Lyssa to an even higher pitch. She felt slender, deft fingers between herself and Savidge, heard another zipper. *My God, she's undressing her boss!*

Lyssa had never felt so decadent. She'd never even *dreamed* of a threesome until she'd been sandwiched between two naked men at the masquerade.

Without releasing his savage hold on her mouth, he lifted her onto the counter. Lyssa felt her slacks being pulled away from her feet. She was so frantic for completion that she eagerly complied when he roughly shoved her knees apart. He lifted one of her legs over his shoulder, forcing her to steady herself by leaning back on her arms. The movement exposed her slit to both boss and admin, but Lyssa was far too aroused to think about blushing. She needed him inside her. *Now.*

He stood immobile, his dark, dark eyes penetrating to her soul, his expression one of intense desire, his breathing a harsh rasp in the quiet room. Still he held back.

"Say it," he ground out.

"Wh—what?" Lyssa couldn't tear her gaze away from his. She was conscious of his hands on her hips, of his cock throbbing hard and hot just inches from her slit, of Andrea toying with her aching, engorged nipples, of the scent of her own juices swirling in the air. Their movements were so coordinated that it was obvious to Lyssa that they'd aided and abetted each other before, and probably not just at the Platinum Society.

"Say it!"

"I want you," she whispered.

"Not right." His grip on her hips tightened into hot pincers.

"I want you to fuck me. Now!" She lifted one hand off the counter and grabbed his hard cock, stroking it, pulling him inexorably closer. "Please, Savidge, please, I want you inside me!"

On a groan, he rammed his cock into her.

She cried out as she felt the thick hardness of him fill her with an inferno of heat that penetrated deep into every cell of her being. With her right leg still over his left shoulder, she braced herself on her arms to withstand his onslaught. But he stood motionless, buried to the hilt inside her, hands gripping her hips until she felt the crescents of his nails digging into her soft flesh. He stared into her eyes, his dark ones piercing deep into hers.

Time stood suspended. She saw a drop of sweat coalesce on his temple. Saw the untamed fire in his eyes, the throbbing of a vein in his neck. Then he withdrew his cock, slowly, inch by scalding inch, until only the tip remained inside her. She murmured her discontent, lifted her pelvis to recapture him.

One side of his mouth tilted up. "What? Tell me. What do you want?"

"Savidge, don't tease me," she whispered breathily. "Please." It came out a sob.

Slowly, inexorably, he pushed his engorged cock partway into her slit.

"Yes," she moaned. "Please…more…"

Once again he rammed all the way in, stayed there, his breath coming fast and hard against the side of her face. Somewhere in a far corner of her consciousness, she heard the door close softly, presumably Andrea leaving, her part in this seduction completed.

"Is this what you want? Like this?"

"Dammit, Savidge, don't tease me!" Lyssa was so hot, so frustrated, she could barely see straight. She squeezed her inner muscles in a frantic attempt to feed her hunger. "Move it!"

He obliged by pulling halfway out again.

With a hiss, Lyssa lifted her left hand from where her fingers had splayed against the cool marble of the counter, and grabbed one tight, round globe of his ass, strained to pull him closer against his token resistance. A devilish grin spread across his handsome face. His eyes sparkled with a lust that made Lyssa's breath stop. Then they darkened, and all trace of playfulness vanished from them.

He moved slowly, pulling back so just the tip of his cock was inside her, then reversed direction unhurriedly, until he was again embedded, his gaze all the while holding hers. He pulled back again, then established a rhythm that gradually gained momentum, ratcheting both of them to a higher and then yet higher plane of sensation, until she was almost incoherent with wanting. Every stroke brought her closer to fever-pitch, until she felt the spasms start, then build, squeezing him, milking him, and ultimately sending her over the edge.

The pace of his movements accelerated as he captured her ecstatic cry with his hot lips, his tongue thrusting into her mouth as vigorously as his cock thrust into her slit.

Lyssa thought she couldn't soar any higher, but the sensuous assault surprised another, stronger orgasm from her, like hurricane waves smashing to the shore one atop the other. Her head lolled back, exposing the long curve of her throat to his devouring mouth as he moved like a hot piston against her.

Suddenly he swore. "I can't believe I forgot—"

With a groan, he pulled out, her name both prayer and curse on his lips.

Lyssa roused herself from a rapturous haze at the sudden withdrawal. She saw his face contort, the muscles and veins in his neck stand out, felt the sudden release of his grip on her hips.

And realized immediately. *No condom.* They'd been too eager, both of them. In a swift, graceful move, she slid her leg down from his shoulder, pushed him back a step, slipped off the counter and sank to her knees. Her hand slid atop his where it gripped the base of his near-to-bursting cock. She guided it into her mouth in time to capture the first throbbing spurts of his semen. She felt him grab a fistful of her hair as he held her head immobile, his hips still pumping, fucking her mouth as he emptied himself into her with a long, guttural cry.

Lyssa tasted her cunt juices on his cock as she sucked him, swallowed his essence, held him in her mouth long after the feral sounds he'd made subsided into jerky, rasping breaths. In a way, she gained comfort from holding him this way, like a baby needs his thumb or his mother's breast to be safe, to be whole. It was an alien feeling to her, but utterly welcome. As though she'd come home.

"Jesus," he croaked. "Lyssa, I'm sorry I had to…"

With her mouth still clasping his deflating cock, she felt him bend down unsteadily and put his hands under her armpits, as if to lift her to her feet. But Lyssa decided she liked the status quo right this minute. With a slight negative shake of her head, she shrugged his hands off and tightened the pressure of her mouth on his cock. She'd never before been the slightest bit curious about a man's anatomy, but somehow it felt right that she should run her tongue around the crown of his cock, feel the smoothness of the jutting ridge, tuck the tip of her tongue inside his opening. She cupped his balls experimentally, learning their texture, soft now and hanging low between his legs, one slightly larger than the other.

Above her, she heard a low moan, and felt her lips stretch into a smile. She'd never known such power over a man before. She tucked her head back, letting the cock slip out of her mouth. It bounced against his balls with a soft *thwap*. She swirled her fingers into the crisp, wiry hairs surrounding its base, marveling at the difference in texture between it and the wavy hair on his head. With an index finger she traced the dark blue vein running along one side of his cock and watched, fascinated, as it twitched and began to swell. She moistened her finger, stroked the vein, glided her finger around the crown. The cock twitched again, swelled to a larger circumference.

"Woman, you're killing me," he growled, and lifted her to her feet in a decisive swoop that left no room for resistance. As soon as she stood erect, he bent down to ravish her mouth in a kiss so torrid that her knees would have buckled without his arms around her in a death grip.

"Jesus," he said when he finally allowed her to come up for air. "What you do to me."

He kissed her eyelids, one after the other, then the tip of her nose, her cheek, her temple. Then tucked her tenderly to his chest. Lyssa closed her eyes, wrapped her arms around his waist, and let the rhythmic thud of his heart beneath her ear soothe her. The heat of him against her torso comforted her like a roaring fireplace on a cold night. She inhaled a deep, bracing breath. And smelled the strong scent of sex, felt the scrape of his chest hair against her naked breasts.

Her eyes popped open. They were both naked, having just fucked like rabbits in the executive washroom on the twenty-first floor of a high-rent Philadelphia office building, and the administrative assistant probably had her ear against the door to discern when she might discreetly knock to remind them that the real world awaited them.

"Savidge." Lyssa shoved him away, her face heating until she was sure she looked like a cooked lobster. He'd transformed her into a greedy, needy lump of hormones and nerve endings every time they crossed paths. She had to put distance between them before she burned to a crisp—or died of embarrassment.

Robert Savidge captured her hands in his and lifted them to his mouth. He kissed her fingertips, each in its turn, before releasing them. "You make a man forget his responsibilities," he murmured. "I'd apologize, but…" He crushed her to his chest, buried his face in her disheveled hair, ran his hands up and down her back. "I can't keep my hands off you."

"Don't," she whispered.

"Don't keep my hands off you?"

"Please," she croaked. "Don't make it worse."

With a resigned sigh he stepped away from her. And tripped, barely managing to keep upright by grabbing onto the marble counter. Looking down, Lyssa realized that his trousers and navy briefs were still pooled around his ankles. Which reminded her of her own nudity. Turning quickly away from the wry look on his face, she shimmied into her own panties and slacks and spied her now-dry bra and shell on top of the ironing board.

"Lyssa, I—"

"Just—go," she said, turning her back to him in a belated show of modesty.

She felt his eyes on her back for a moment, then heard the door open. Before it closed again, she heard him say, "Here, you might want this."

Only after she heard the door close did she turn around. He had thoughtfully set her purse on the counter.

Lyssa closed her eyes. She had to get far away from him, as fast as she could. Or she might find herself falling for such a sensitive, perceptive man who could turn her brain into cooked oatmeal and her knees to mashed potatoes.

Chapter Five

"You're not running away again."

Lyssa felt trapped. She'd opened the washroom door a crack to see if she could escape without further embarrassment, and there he was, waiting for her, looking sexy and sophisticated and totally at ease. For long moments as she'd combed her hair and repaired her makeup, she stared at the stranger looking back at her from the washroom mirror. She'd turned into an odalisque, lusting after a man she'd only met a few days ago.

What must he think of her? It couldn't be any worse than her own low opinion of herself, acting like a bitch in heat or worse, a nymphomaniac who so easily succumbed to the first man who tried to seduce her.

No, that wasn't fair. Other men had pursued her at the Platinum Society, but she'd turned them away. It was Robert Savidge she'd chosen to seduce with her dance, and he simply took what she offered. And, damn, she *had* been in heat. Had been consumed with satisfying the raging hormones she hadn't known she possessed over the many unhappy years of her marriage. How could she blame Savidge? After all, they'd met at an orgy, for heaven's sake.

She wondered if she'd ever be able to accept that earthier side of herself. Just how earthy she'd been had scared the daylights out of her.

"Please, Lyssa, hear me out." Robert Savidge stood in the anteroom a non-threatening distance from her. He gestured to one of the wing chairs they'd sat in before, indicating he wanted her to sit down and continue their attorney-client chat as if they hadn't just rubbed bellies to a volcanic explosion a few minutes ago.

Lyssa stood her ground in the doorway, her teeth clenched.

Soft piano music wafted through hidden speakers. Yanni, she thought. Soothing, New Age music meant to calm. She had no intention of calming down. Robert Savidge could take his randy appendage and shove it in the nearest pencil sharpener. She would not, would *not*, be just a handy receptacle for his lust.

"If you could give me the confirmation number," she said, trying to put frost and disdain into her voice, "I'll be on my way. We still have last-minute packing to do. We're leaving at seven tomorrow morning for Dartmouth."

"Lyssa—" her name fell like warm cognac from his mouth, "—we have to talk about it."

She lifted her chin in defiance. Her mouth thinned to a tight line.

He took a step toward her. She tensed.

"Lyssa," he tried again, "try to see it from my point of view. You came to my father's home Saturday night, to an orgy sponsored by the Platinum Society, which, in blunt language, is a sex club. You came as the guest of a long-time member, Kathryn Ondov Donaldson. You mingled freely with the guests, allowed men to touch you, to rub their naked bodies against you. You performed a dance of incredible sensuousness, divesting yourself of all your clothes, flimsy as they were, seeing as how they were nothing but a handful of diaphanous veils, and flung yourself naked into my very aroused lap. You spread your legs and allowed, no, you *reveled* in my mouth on your cunt. The next day you came to my office—"

"I didn't know I'd run into *you*," she spat the pronoun as though a cockroach had found its way into her mouth.

"—to my office," he ran roughshod over her protest, "and melted as soon as I touched you. You wrapped your legs around me and couldn't get enough of my kisses. You wanted me as much as I wanted you when I fucked you on my desk.

"Today, Andrea told you she'd seen you at the masquerade and, if I'm not mistaken, showed you the eagle feather tattooed on her breast, but you had already admired it that night, admired her breasts, in fact, hadn't you? And you didn't protest, didn't stop her when she started kissing those rosy nipples of yours."

Lyssa gasped. "You *watched?* Before...before you came into the washroom?"

He took another step closer, his predatory grin answering her question. She stood her ground.

"And did you stop to protest when each of us had one of your breasts in hand?" he continued relentlessly. "Or when Andrea pulled down your pants? Or when you demanded that I fuck you? Or when you grabbed my ass to get me closer? I don't have to remind you that when I belatedly had the presence of mind to pull out because I wasn't wearing a condom, you went down on—"

"Stop!" Lyssa squeezed her eyes shut and pressed her palms against her ears. They felt as hot as her face. "You make me sound like a nymphomaniac."

"Lyssa," he said gently, "I'm not trying to embarrass you. I just stated the facts as I saw them. What I saw was a beautiful, sensual woman who was proud to display her knockout body, a woman who, for some inexplicable reason, chose me out of all the men at the party to offer herself to. Do you blame me for coming back to the well for more?"

His voice sounded close to her. Slowly Lyssa let her hands slide down from her ears, opened her eyes. Robert Savidge stood before her, hands casually in his pants pockets, white shirt with the top two buttons unbuttoned, tie hanging loose around his neck.

She lowered her gaze to the parquet floor, idly letting her eyes pick out the intricate pattern of the wood. Her mouth felt dried out, like a cake that had been in the oven an hour too long. "The way you said it sounds..."

Sordid. She worried her lower lip. "Please. Let me go. I can't allow myself to think about anything but my daughter. I'm driving her to New Hampshire tomorrow. I'll be saying goodbye to my little girl and when she comes back for Thanksgiving weekend, she'll be all grown up. I can't take any more emotion right now. Please." She raised her eyes to his. "Just give me the confirmation number so I can go home and tell her everything's all right."

After a long pause, Robert Savidge swore softly and turned away. "Coming right up."

Chapter Six

"Oh, good. You made yourself at home. Have you been waiting long?"

Lyssa opened her eyes and half turned in the lounge chair. Kat bustled onto the patio carrying a lacquered tray holding a wine bottle and two long-stemmed glasses.

"I got here about four-thirty." It was now after six on Saturday afternoon. The air was sultry, the sun tipping behind the tall oak trees in Kat's backyard. Nary a ripple disturbed the surface of the amoeba-shaped pool. "It felt good to have absolutely nothing to decide for two hours except whether I wanted to jump in and get my hair wet or to stay absolutely immobile in the sun and doze."

Kat chuckled. "I can see by the damp ponytail that you actually made a decision."

Lyssa lifted her hand to the haphazardly arranged blonde locks inside a scrunchie. "It's almost dry again. Honest, Kat, I can't believe getting one young lady off to school could leave such a mess behind. I spent the whole day straightening up the house."

"You had quite a week," Kat observed. "A nine-hour drive up, a day settling Michelle at school, nine hours back and bingo, your vacation's gone." She set down the tray on a small wrought-iron table between two chairs. "Here. Make yourself useful and open the wine while I get out of my work clothes. We'll have a dip before I dish the food."

"I lifted the lid. That lamb stew smells heavenly. I've never used a slow cooker."

"You're not that organized," Kat retorted. "You'd have to do the peeling, browning, and so forth in the morning in order to eat that night."

"Very funny." Lyssa sat up and reached for corkscrew and bottle. "Mmm. Chilean Merlot. What are we celebrating?"

"I'll offer a toast in a minute. Just pop the cork."

A few minutes later Kat returned and flopped on the adjacent lounge chair. Lyssa thought Kat's skimpy red bikini showed off her tall, curvy figure to perfection. Lyssa herself wore a backless, white maillot with high-cut legs and a neckline that plunged down to her waist, with a modesty hook at her breast that she'd left undone. She'd bought it at Kat's insistence but had never worn it before. After her torrid encounters with Robert Savidge, she was starting to feel as though she could be—or rather, was—sexy.

Lyssa filled each glass half full. Notes of cherry and oak swirled from the bowl to her nose as she poured. They clinked glasses. "What are we drinking to?"

"Sex, what else?" Kat laughed, the sound low and sexy.

"Well, um…"

"Come on, Lyssa. Dish. You had that gladiator tied in knots. Honestly, you could almost *see* the sparks fly between you. First he devours you with his eyes, then with his—"

"Stop." Dammit, her cheeks were getting hot again.

Kat sat up, leaned an arm on the table between them. "Lyssa, this is me you're talking to. Your best friend, your maid of honor, your daughter's godmother, the one who stood beside you when that jerk was screwing around on you.

"I'll let you in on a secret. That's the first time I've seen him really get into it. You've done something a lot of women in the club would give up their botox injections for. You got him to *participate*."

"But--but—" Despite her reticence to talk about Robert Savidge, Lyssa felt a warmth spread throughout her body at her friend's comment. "He never—? But wasn't that his father's house? How long have you known him?"

"Years. His wife used to drop a lot of money at the gallery. Of course, that was before I owned it. Then when he joined Quick, Bowers, I hung the two oils in his office. The man has excellent taste in art."

Lyssa heard nothing after *his wife*. Robert Savidge was married? Oh God, how could she have done what she'd done with a married man? And Kat didn't even know about the quickie in his office. To say nothing of the threebie in the executive washroom. Her face flamed.

"Oooooh, talk to me, Lyssa! You're remembering something absolutely delish!"

"Married?" It came out no more than a croak.

"Lyss, half the people at the club are married. They get their kicks by fucking in public, or by swapping spouses, by watching, or by who knows what."

"But I would *never* have done anything if I'd known he was—"

"Hello, Earth to Lyssa, the fireman and the cowboy who made the Lyssa sandwich? Both of those guys had their wives watching while they rubbed your bacon."

Lyssa dropped her head into her hands. "I'm so sorry..."

"No need to be sorry, dear heart. Word is both of the wives were pleased with the fallout."

"Fallout?" The word came out timid, muffled, through Lyssa's palms.

"Yeah. Mo told me her hubby hadn't been so horny in months after you turned him on. And Stacey, well, Stacey was ready to jump you herself after watching Eric with you. Eric was the fireman in the yellow slicker." Kat chuckled. "She had no complaints by the end of the night, either."

For a moment Lyssa sat, elbows on knees, bowed head in her hands, absorbing the implications. Those men and their wives had thought she was a turn-on. Two couples had reaped the benefit of what they had perceived as her sexuality. Add Andrea to the head count and she was coming to the conclusion that it had been George, not her, whose sexual needle was stuck on empty.

Then she remembered. Robert Savidge's wife. Her head jerked up. "You said Savidge is married? Was his wife there? How did she react?"

Kat laughed as she poured more wine into her glass. "Did I say that? Yeah, he was married, once upon a time. They've been divorced, oh, must be six or seven years by now."

Lyssa's shoulders sagged in relief. She, who had been so hurt when George had violated their marriage vows, wouldn't be responsible for perpetrating the same kind of hurt on another unsuspecting spouse.

She took a small sip of wine. "You said he never participated before?"

"Honey, it's a wonder you didn't bleed from all the daggers you got when he went down on you. He's gorgeous, rich, smart, and tantalizingly aloof. Every female member—and some of the males—had tried to get him to put out."

"But why would he come to these, uh, affairs if he didn't participate?"

"Don't forget the venue. His father's house. Robert felt obligated to be like a majordomo. You know. Making sure everyone had fun, was comfortable with what was happening to them, that things didn't get out of hand. If someone was being whipped, say, he had to decide whether they *wanted* to be whipped. That's what makes this such a great club. Everyone can explore whatever proclivities they discover they have and still feel safe."

"Oh."

"And I just *knew* you were right for him."

The beginnings of a smile curved Lyssa's mouth upward. "So you played cupid and invited me to see what would happen?"

"Something like that." Kat's expression looked like a smug cat that had just licked a bowl of cream empty.

"What about his administrative assistant?"

"Andrea? She and her husband are members, too. You saw them in action. Remember the woman who tied the Indian's hands to the table and tortured him with a feather from her own headdress?"

Lyssa didn't want to ask, but it just tripped out of her mouth. "Does she, uh, do anything with her boss?"

"I'm sure there's some priming of the pump, but she's totally over the moon about her hubby, if you're worried. Most of the members 'help'—" Kat made quotations with her fingers, " — each other on occasion. Sometimes two hands just aren't enough." She gave Lyssa a penetrating look. "Why? Did something happen that I should know about?"

A ringing phone interrupted them. With no little relief at not having to answer that particular question about Andrea and her boss, Lyssa reached into the canvas bag at her feet and rummaged around its contents. She pulled the gadget out and checked the readout. "Ick. That's George. He doesn't have my cell phone number. He must have called my home. I call-forwarded in case Michelle tries to reach me." She sighed. "I guess I have to talk to him sooner or later. Do you mind?"

"No, not at all. I'll get dinner set up."

As Kat discreetly moved into the house, Lyssa pressed the Open button.

"What do you mean, calling my house like a harpy and scaring the hell out of SueAnn?"

"And hello to you, too, George."

"I'm not kidding, Lyssa. What are you trying to do?"

"Who's SueAnn?"

"MariBeth's sister. And stop trying to change the subject. Why are you threatening me?"

Lyssa gritted her teeth. "I did no such thing. I merely had an emergency regarding your daughter and I needed to talk to you urgently."

"Well, I'm here. Talk."

Take a deep breath, Lyssa. Don't let him get to you. She put all the scorn she could into her voice. "The emergency was last Monday. For your information, today is Saturday.

I couldn't wait a whole week for you to condescend to call back. I handled it myself."

"Come on, get real. You? Handled an emergency? How did you do that, by calling the fire department?" His chuckle grated on Lyssa's ears.

"I refuse to let you rile me."

"What was this big emergency, anyway?"

"I don't have time to talk. I'm at Kat's and we're having a party. I'll get back to you some time next week." She disconnected the call and tossed the phone back into her bag.

"Bravo!" Kat stood at the patio door, a large earthenware bowl in her hands.

"I can't believe I ever thought I loved that jerk. Do you need help?"

"No, just sit. I've got everything under control." Somewhere inside the house, the phone rang. Kat rolled her eyes. "If it's that asshole—" She turned and went back in, taking the bowl with her. "I'll fix that little peckerhead."

Lyssa could hear her friend's raised voice in the kitchen. It had to be George, judging from Kat's scathing comments. Tension coiled a tight knot in her gut. He was even worse now than when they were going through the divorce. She strode to the pool and dove in. The warm water caressed her, soothed her. She did a butterfly stroke to the deep end, then turned onto her back and floated, arms out, eyes closed, trying to purge herself of negative thoughts. She would *not* let him rule her emotions.

Water splashed over her face. Lyssa sputtered, opened her eyes. Kat had jumped into the pool like a cannonball. She surfaced, spat water then let out a howl of laughter. "I fixed his skinny ass. I told him you were having a torrid affair with a billionaire."

"Kat, you didn't!" In spite of her lingering doubts that George would believe her friend, Lyssa laughed. Then her demeanor sobered. "I suppose his lawyer will tell him what we did. But I'll still have to talk to him myself. He can rake me over the coals, but I won't let him do this to Michelle."

Kat stroked her way to the shallow end of the pool. "Come on, let's tackle that lamb stew." She scrambled up the three steps and, unhooking her bra-top and tossing it on a chaise, reached for a towel.

Lyssa followed her out of the water, laughing as she realized one of her straps had slipped down her shoulder from the force of Kat's cannonball entry, baring one breast to the warmth of the setting sun. She shrugged the remaining strap down the other shoulder and stood, arms outstretched as if to encompass the world, face raised to the deepening sky. A gentle breeze sent goose bumps skittering across her damp flesh. "I am the goddess of the setting sun," she intoned. "I command my subjects to toss all their offal at George Markham."

"I kneel at your feet, Goddess of the Setting Sun."

Lyssa's head snapped around. Robert Savidge strode toward her, wearing tan linen slacks and a sky-blue knitted polo shirt. With long fingers he encircled her outstretched wrists and brought them together as he knelt before her. The action brought her breasts to more fullness, enhancing her cleavage and thrusting the nipples out to him. She could feel her face flaming to have her friend see her in her backyard, in full daylight, her nearly naked body shimmering with drops of water in the presence of the fully clothed man who had turned her into a purely sexual being. Against her will, her nipples tightened and heat curled in her lower belly, spreading to the center of exquisite sensation that he already knew so well.

"What—" Her voice came out an octave too high. She cleared her throat. "What are you doing here?"

"I caught a whiff the most enticing, delicious scent…"

She tried subtly, and futilely, to remove her hands from his firm grip. Not for the first time in Robert Savidge's presence, she silently cursed her inability to stop a blush. "Y-yes, Kat's lamb stew is to die for."

His soft laugh sent ripples of pleasure up her spine. "That's not the scent that captured me, Goddess." He leaned closer, his eyes level with her belly button. His warm breath puffed out in a soft cloud against her skin. "It's somewhere around here…"

"Don't, please don't." Less subtly now, she pulled hard against his grip as she backed away a step.

In a single swift motion, he stood up and swept his arms around her, pressing her wet body against his crisp clothing. His lips found and captured hers in a kiss that was unexpectedly gentle, almost nurturing. "I missed you," he growled, his mouth brushing against her cheek.

"Okay, folks, stop that fooling around before I get jealous. Dinner's ready."

At Kat's interruption, Savidge released her. Gratefully, Lyssa slipped her straps back up, leaning forward to settle her full breasts into the bra-cups. She fumbled with the hook in the center of the plunging Vee, but his hand on hers stayed her.

"Don't," he whispered. "I want to fantasize that something might pop out while we're eating dinner." His eyes bored into hers, promising to make his fantasies come true.

The intensity of his gaze shot tingles to every inch of her skin. She broke the gaze first, lowering her eyes. Then let out a small cry of dismay. "Your shirt is all wet."

Devilish smile tilting one side of his mouth, he shrugged. "It's cotton. The pants are linen. All natural. They'll dry." He pulled out a padded, wrought-iron chair for her at the round patio table and gestured for her to sit.

"Where is she?" George Markham stalked around the side of the house and onto the patio. "There you are. How dare you hang up on me? You tell me my daughter has an emergency and then blithely say you're at a party and can't be bothered to discuss it?"

Halted in the act of sitting down, Lyssa straightened her knees and spine, thrust out her chin. She scrutinized the man she'd been married to for nineteen years, noting the thinning brownish hair, the big ears, the slight paunch he tried to disguise by wearing a sport shirt over baggy shorts. "That emergency is old news, George. I told you, I took care of it."

"I demand to know what was so important that you had to upset my wife and disrupt my honeymoon. "

"Your—" The breath whooshed out of Lyssa. She didn't care, she really didn't, whether he'd gotten married. It was just…what would Michelle think? He was her *father*. Would he just spring that bit of news on her the same insensitive way he'd just poleaxed Lyssa herself?

"Robert Savidge," she heard the taller, more elegant man beside her say. "Of Quick, Bowers & Savidge." He extended his hand to George. "I'm the senior partner who handled Jack Bowers' little problem that Mrs. Markham brought to my attention."

George looked at the outstretched hand as though it was a snake baring venom-tipped fangs. "What kind of problem could Jack Bowers have that concerns my ex?"

"A little matter of tuition for your daughter." Savidge lowered his hand.

"Oh, they allow late matriculation all the time. Don't worry, I'll take care of it."

"She's your daughter," Lyssa said, striving hard to keep her temper from erupting. "And you're responsible for her education. The divorce decree specifically states that you are to pay for her tuition in a timely manner."

George waved his hand in dismissal. "Timely means when I can sell my stocks without taking a bath."

"Timely," Savidge inserted smoothly, "means on time. It means payment made prior to the deadline, which in this case was Tuesday last. You are in default of your divorce agreement and I am in the process of drawing up papers—"

"You're not my lawyer. Jack is."

Savidge continued as though he hadn't been interrupted. "—papers that will inform you as to steps taken by Quick, Bowers & Savidge to minimize said default."

George narrowed his eyes. "What do you mean?"

"I mean, sir, that the law firm you retained as trustee of your daughter's trust fund has a fiduciary obligation to the beneficiary of said trust fund as well as to the client. One advantage of a large law firm is that when one attorney is engaged in a lengthy trial, as Jack Bowers was this week, another attorney in said firm will step in to perform any and all necessary services on behalf of the client. As the senior partner covering Jack's caseload, I have taken steps to mitigate the losses your daughter's trust fund might suffer by your reneging on the terms of the divorce decree."

"What losses?" George sputtered. "There wasn't a thing in that decree—"

"Legal fees in the event that Mrs. Markham sues the trust for nonperformance."

"You conniving little bitch!" George spun around to face Lyssa, who had been marveling, openmouthed, at the change in Robert Savidge from sexually proficient dilettante to razor-sharp lawyer. "You think you can pull one over on me?" He took a step toward her, his furious gaze raking her from her damp ponytail to the unhooked top of her swimsuit to her red-painted toenails.

In spite of her resolve, Lyssa found herself backing up a step at his vituperative words.

"You don't get your way, you try to hit me in the wallet, is that it?"

Lyssa forced herself to meet George's disdainful stare. "I never really knew you," she choked out. "This is your *daughter* we're talking about."

"No, it isn't. It's about you trying to get more money out of me, trying to destroy me because you didn't manage to walk away from this disaster of a marriage with my Bentley and my portfolio and the shirt off my back."

"Destroy you? I just want to disassociate myself from you. And it would have worked if you hadn't pulled this stunt against your own flesh and blood." Lyssa squared her shoulders, plunked tightly closed fists on her hips, and took a deep breath. "If I never see you—"

George's gaze snapped down to her breasts. The breasts she'd left vulnerable to view by not hooking the clasp holding the top of her swimsuit in place. From her peripheral vision Lyssa noted that the swaths of nylon and spandex barely covered her nipples. Belatedly she realized that her hands-on-hips motion had only enhanced the ripe fullness of her breasts, jutting them up and forward, exposing them to view, the nipples tautening under the swish of the flimsy material.

"You—you—whore!" George flicked his stare from her breasts to Savidge, then back again, as though he couldn't keep away from the luscious view. "You seduced him into this. Jack Bowers would never have put me in such an untenable position."

In spite of her anger at her ex, Lyssa felt a laugh bubbling up from deep within, a loud, hearty belly laugh that left George looking nonplussed.

"Oh, George, you should see your face," she choked out when she regained her breath. "All through our marriage you made me feel as though I was frigid, that I was a fat cow, that no one, least of all you, would want me." She pulled in another deep breath, heedless of the fact that the Lycra slid back to expose more of her skin, and chuckled. "And now you're accusing me of using that same frigid, fat-cow body to seduce a man like Robert Savidge? A man that half the women in Philadelphia would give up their Rolls Royces for?"

George scowled, then shrugged. "Some men like them plump."

That started Lyssa laughing again. "Yes, indeed. I found that out the other night when four, no, wait, I think maybe it was five, yes, five gentlemen propositioned me."

"Yeah, right." George's face darkened.

"Let's see if I remember this correctly." She brought a closed hand up, unwinding a finger with each enumeration. "One was wearing a kilt, and you know Scotsmen don't wear anything underneath them—I learned that for a fact that night. One wore a fireman's slicker, unbuttoned, of course. Hmmm, he must have been a Scot, too, because he wasn't wearing anything underneath except a hard...um," she cleared her throat, "...never mind. There was also a pasha and a gladiator and..."

"Don't forget the Indian," she heard Kat say behind her.

"Mmmm, as if could I forget how his loincloth tented up as he lay helpless with his wrists bound to the table legs. Oh yes, and I noticed how the naked man handcuffed to a hook in the ceiling followed me with his eyes..."

Her head bobbed as George grabbed her by the shoulders and shook her. "You're just trying to get even," he snarled. "Where did you suddenly get such an imagination? For years all you did was lay there like a lump when I fucked you and now you're trying to convince me you're a hot swinger?"

Lyssa pointedly looked at his hands gripping her shoulders. "Don't bruise the merchandise, bub. They're waiting in line to run their lips down that smooth skin of mine and I don't want it marred in any way."

He let go as if his fingers had suddenly been burned, and staggered back a step. "You've changed."

Lyssa was pleased to hear his voice had turned hoarse. "Yes, I've changed. Thank heaven." A smile playing around the corners of her mouth, she sidled over to where Robert Savidge stood, his stance tense and expectant, as if ready to come to her rescue should the need arise. She positioned herself in front of him, her back to his chest, then reached behind her to place her palms on the firm butt cheeks she loved to squeeze, and slowly began to gyrate her hips.

She was gratified to hear Savidge's quick intake of breath. For a moment he stood statue-still. Her breath came quicker as she felt his cock swell inside those linen trousers. She leaned back until her whole body brushed against him, thrusting her breasts out in invitation.

It didn't take long for Savidge to accept it. From behind, he placed his large hands on her waist, splaying his fingers until their tips encountered the undersides of her breasts. He caressed the curved flesh, nudging his fingers underneath the Lycra strips, edging upward to her nipples, which had tightened to unbearably hard points. He dipped his head to nuzzle the back of her neck, then her ear. She felt the scrape of his teeth on her lobe and let out a soft, involuntary mewling sound.

She closed her eyes and reveled in the wickedness of it, the handsome, formidable man arousing her in full view of the ex-husband who'd convinced himself she was sexless and frigid. She felt Savidge's fingers tweaking her nipples, heard his breath quicken as he rubbed his steel-hard cock against the small of her back.

Lazily she opened her eyes and looked at the man who'd spent nineteen years not bothering to discover who she was. She pulled off the scrunchie and threaded her fingers through her blonde hair, letting it sift down to her shoulders in a slow waterfall. "Go home, George. Go to your nubile young bride and see if she can satisfy you. Thank you for giving me Michelle. As for the rest…"

Deliberately she turned her back on George Markham and lifted her face to Robert Savidge. Standing on tiptoe, she invited his kiss. Savidge's arms came around her, clamping her to the hard length of him, his hands stroking up and down her naked back. His lips claimed hers in a fiery kiss that she welcomed openmouthed.

And all thoughts of her ex fled.

Chapter Seven

"Oh, Lyss, I thought his eyeballs were going to burst!"

Lyssa smiled at her friend's exaggeration but admitted, "I don't think I've ever seen him speechless before."

Still, the thought of George goggling at her uninhibited actions made Lyssa's mouth curve upward even more. Seeing him stalking off the patio and around the side of Kat's house prompted the thought, *good riddance.* His ridiculous behavior had provoked her to shock him, and she wasn't the least bit repentant.

The remaining threesome had dined on Kat's excellent lamb stew and now sat at her dining room table finishing that superb Merlot. She still wasn't comfortable baring her all in front of mixed company, so she'd convinced Kat to join her in donning shorts and tees.

Lyssa swirled the wine around in her glass, took a slow sip, and gazed over the rim at Robert Savidge seated across from her. His penetrating stare sizzled all the way through her body and made her bare feet curl into the soft carpeting.

"Thank you for going along with the flow," she said.

"My pleasure."

The silk in his voice made her eyelashes flutter downward. Just how much pleasure, she'd already experienced. Several times. She felt the telltale heat of a blush creeping up her neck. And she wanted more. How could this one man have transformed her, in less than a week, into an insatiable, wanton woman when she'd had only occasional, mildly satisfying sexual encounters over the past many years of marriage?

She realized she was stroking her throat and down to her shoulder inside the neckline of her tee. Her body language must be sending a vivid message. With an effort she lowered her hand to her side. She would *not* beg. She was *not* a nymphomaniac. This wasn't a lifetime commitment; she was just trying out her wings. She simply found Robert Savidge…irresistible, and had subconsciously wished for his hand, his lips, to be stroking her.

"He's one of our more difficult clients, I'm told."

Lyssa snapped her attention to Savidge's comment.

"He was pretty difficult to live with the past few years, too," Kat offered. "I can't tell you how many times Lyssa came over for coffee and a shoulder to cry on."

"Can we talk about something else?" Lyssa's voice was subdued but forceful. Savidge did *not* need to know all about her failed marriage. "I'd like to look toward the future, not the past."

Kat chortled. "Yeah, like going back to work tomorrow."

Savidge focused laser-sharp eyes on her. "Tomorrow? Sunday?"

"The real estate market hums on Sundays. Lots of open houses, lots of browsers. I'm low man on the totem pole," she explained ruefully, "so I had to promise to work the next three weekends in exchange for getting a high-demand vacation week to get Michelle off to school. My license isn't even a year old."

"Yeah, she had to wait until after that prick took his fat thumb off her and she was actually able to take the course," Kat finished for her. "Passed the exam first time out, too."

Lyssa shot her friend an annoyed look. She didn't want anyone airing her dirty linen in public.

"What does George do for a living?" Savidge asked. "I don't remember seeing anything in the file."

"He's an investment counselor." She named the Philadelphia office of a nationally known brokerage firm. "He always bragged how he conned this one or that one to buy some stock or other, then convinced them to sell shortly thereafter, gloating that he got a hefty commission both buying and selling."

"Sounds like a churner."

She tossed a questioning look at Savidge.

"A churner is someone who buys and sells other people's stocks too quickly, for just that reason. Even though the client might make a small profit on the sale, the only sure thing is that the broker gets his commission." Savidge poured the last of the wine into his glass. "Maybe someone in the SEC would be interested."

"Oh no, I don't want to make trouble for him. I just want him out of my life."

Savidge aimed a devastatingly sexy smile at her. "Let me know if you change your mind."

They lingered over coffee, the three of them. Lyssa was loath to make the first move to leave. On the one hand, she enjoyed the company, the conversation, especially his expertise on a wide range of subjects. As the saying went, he'd been there, done that. So many things, so many places, that she was jealous. Sailing the Atlantic coast in an 1840s schooner, hiking the Appalachian trail, white-water rafting the Colorado River, cross-country skiing in Vail, the kinds of things she'd wanted to try but George had insisted on spending vacations at Cape Cod, vegetating in a beach chair with his cell phone glued to his ear.

On the other hand, wasn't she waiting for the teeniest hint that Savidge would invite her to his home for a night of mind-blowing sex?

Somewhere in the house, Kat's prized grandfather clock chimed. Lyssa counted the strokes silently. Dismayed, she thought, *midnight already*? She had to be at the real estate office at ten, and she was still exhausted from her frenzied week of getting Michelle off to college. Why hadn't he said anything, hinted his desire with a look or a word?

Lyssa finally pushed her chair out and stood. "I think I'm going to turn into a pumpkin if I don't get home soon."

Savidge stood as well. "I'll walk you to your car."

The sudden heaviness in her legs made walking an effort. She was going to go home alone. Amazed at how disappointed she was, she picked up her dirty plate and silverware and brought it to the kitchen. Her eyes met Kat's. "Thanks for everything. It was delicious."

Kat acknowledged the compliment with a nod. Her eyes seemed to sparkle as she tossed a glance to Savidge.

Abruptly Lyssa's stomach took a dive. That secret look...how could she have been so stupid, so blind? Both of them had been waiting for her to leave before they could jump each other's bones!

Well, of course. After all, Kat and Savidge had known each other for years, had been in the same sex club together, had coupled who knows how many times before she, Lyssa, had even entered the picture. And who wouldn't want Kat—tall, willowy, sophisticated, *experienced* Kat?

Shoulders squared, Lyssa said to him, "It's okay, you don't have to bother. It's right at the curb."

"It's no bother at all." The low timbre of his voice reached down into Lyssa's core and made her tingle. And made her furious that he could still affect her that way, even though right now she felt like a fifth wheel. Okay, so she'd allowed strangers to paw her, and yes, excite her, but Robert Savidge had touched something deep inside her that made her feel like a tightly budded rose about to blossom.

But now, all she could feel were the thorns.

Seemingly unperturbed at her sudden cool attitude, he took her by the elbow and walked her down Kat's hallway. He opened the front door for her and followed her down the steps to the curb, where her Honda was parked. She pulled the keys out of her purse and felt them being tugged out of her hand.

"Lyssa," he whispered, spinning her around so her back was to the car. He pinned her between his warm, rangy body and the cool metal of the SUV. His mouth descended on hers in a bruising, feral kiss. Although it left her knees weak, she would not give him the satisfaction of showing it. Her arms remained at her sides, but her mouth softened, opened against his sensual onslaught.

"Get in," he rasped, pulling away abruptly and bending down to unlock her door.

His kiss had made her eyes cross. She mentally shook herself, wondering how he could play two women at the same time, and how she could react that way even knowing he'd done so. Sliding into the bucket seat, she reached out with open palm for the keys and snatched her hand away as soon as they fell into her grasp. She pulled the door shut behind her and refused to roll down the window.

It took her three tries before she was able to fit the key into the ignition. To make up for it, she floored the accelerator and laid down a trail of rubber behind her.

Hours later, lying awake in her big, lonely bed, Lyssa stared at the dim ceiling and wondered when she'd become such a fool. It was only a fling, she kept telling herself. It wasn't as though she was falling in love with him. She had no claim on him. None whatsoever.

Then why did it hurt so?

* * * * *

The home that popped up on the screen was a brick-faced Tudor with an overhanging second floor and several roof lines. "Here it is. Twenty-seven Ashleigh Lane. Four bedrooms, three and a half baths, kitchen updated last year, new slate roof, professional landscaping." Lyssa rattled off statistics to the woman on the other end of the phone, paused for a question, scrolled down to find the answer. "The taxes are fourteen thousand five hundred dollars.

"Yes, that's for a year." She had a feeling that the woman was just window-shopping, but as the potential selling agent, she was polite and enthusiastic even though part of her mind remained with Robert Savidge. Had he spent the night with Kat? Had he made her scream when she came? How many times did they do it?

"I'm sorry, could you repeat that?"

The woman, a Mrs. Peifer, wanted to see the home. "Let me call the owners to let them know I'll be bringing a visitor. Is three o'clock good for you?"

Reluctantly, Lyssa agreed to five p.m. at the woman's insistence. She only worked to six, and hoped the woman wouldn't take too much longer than that. Still, the possibility of a commission on a three-quarters-of-a-million-dollar sale could tempt her to work late. Anyway, it wasn't as if she had someone to go home to.

She rang off, then made the arrangements, and was setting the phone back in its cradle when the door opened. She couldn't see who entered, because he/she was hidden behind an enormous vase of red roses. Someone must have paid a pretty penny to get a Sunday delivery, she mused.

A head peeked out from behind the veritable garden. "Delivery for Ms. Lyssa Markham. Where do you want me to set it?"

"For m-me?" She'd been sure it would be for one of the other two women behind their computers, the older one, whose husband was always surprising her with things, and the other, younger one, who changed boyfriends as often as she changed her shoes. Lyssa cleared her throat and scrambled to her feet. "Uh, here," she said, hastily clearing a corner of her desk of its papers.

The young man set down his burden and stood at her desk, shuffling his feet. Belatedly Lyssa realized he probably wanted a tip. And well he should, with such a delivery, she thought wryly. She pulled a few bills from her purse and handed them over the desk, then immediately forgot about him.

There was a card.

With trembling fingers she opened the envelope. In a bold, scrawling hand, it read, "They remind me of you. R."

"Robert," she murmured.

"Oooh," the older woman squealed. "What did you have to do for *that*?"

"Evann, hush," the other reprimanded. "I'll bet Lyssa has men falling at her feet all the time."

Fifty-year-old Evann would not be hushed. "Who's Robert? What's the occasion?"

Lyssa reached her hand out to touch the velvety, blood-red petals, noting that the stems had been de-thorned. Several flowers were half open, some were in full bloom, and many were still tightly budded. Which ones reminded Savidge of her? The ones just unfolding, as she had done under his expert tutelage? The velvety texture of her slit that he'd felt with his tongue? The fully open welcome her body had given him?

Feeling the start of a blush at her thoughts, Lyssa turned from her audience. "He's just the friend of a friend."

"Yeah, right."

Lyssa was prevented from responding by the entrance of another potential client. Evann took the caller to her desk, and that was the end of the prying. She hoped.

At ten of five, Lyssa closed out her computer and straightened her desk. The client, a trim, stylish woman wearing a classic Dior linen suit, arrived right on time. She appeared to be, as the saying went, "of an age", which could be anywhere from forty to seventy, but well turned out.

As she escorted Mrs. Peifer outside, the woman asked, "Do you mind if I drive?"

Frowning at the deviation from normal, Lyssa hesitated only a moment, feeling ridiculous to have briefly thought that the client might kidnap her, then followed the woman to a long, black Lexus.

"I have this phobia, you see," she explained. "I'm deathly afraid of the shotgun seat."

Lyssa bit back a smile. "There was plenty of room in the back seat of my Honda. We don't usually have the client do the work." Settling into the passenger seat, she glanced at the clipboard with her paperwork, intending to give Mrs. Peifer directions.

The older woman apparently knew exactly where she was going, signaling with her blinker before Lyssa had time to tell her. But instead of stopping at twenty-seven Ashleigh Lane, she continued past it and turned right at the next corner. Several blocks and another turn later, she drove up a serpentine driveway bisecting a lawn as smooth and green as a golf course and edged with flowerbeds in full bloom, looking for all the world like an English nobleman's country estate smack in the middle of Devon.

"Mrs. Peifer—?" Lyssa started to question.

"I hope you don't mind, dear. I definitely want to see that house we discussed, and we'll go back. But since we're in the area, I thought you should see this house first. It's going to be put on the market soon. Maybe you can get the listing. The owner is a dear friend of mine and he happens to be home this afternoon—just before I left, I called to make sure. You know, he's so hard to pin down, what with all his business trips and the like. I'm a firm believer in making hay while the sun shines."

"Well, if he's expecting us…"

"Now didn't I just say so?" Mrs. Peifer parked in front of an imposing entranceway to a three-story brick manor house, set the brake and turned off the ignition. She glanced at Lyssa and gave her a disarming smile as they got out of the car.

Okay, Lyssa thought. *All in a day's work.*

They climbed wide front steps to a portico, and when they reached the massive oak door, Mrs. Peifer rapped the distinctive lion's-head knocker. A tall, ropy man with Oriental features answered. "Good afternoon, Mrs. P," he said. "Come in. He's in the kitchen, overseeing my cooking, as usual."

"Thank you, Yuki."

Lyssa followed Mrs. Peifer into a wide front hallway with a spacious, richly appointed living room off to one side and dining room on the other. The aroma of something meaty and delicious wafted through an open archway and they followed the smell.

They entered a well-equipped kitchen with leaded-glass inserts in the cupboard doors. Lyssa's breath whooshed out at the sight of the man stirring the saucepan at the restaurant-grade range. It looked like—

He turned. It was Savidge. Her knees threatened to give out. He raised a hand in greeting. "Hey, Charlene."

"Hello, Robert." He and Mrs. Peifer grasped hands like old friends.

Lyssa's head snapped from one to the other, as though she were watching a tennis match. She refused to take note of how attractive he looked in form-fitting black slacks and ice-blue shirt, long sleeves rolled up to his elbows, top two buttons casually unbuttoned to reveal a thatch of black hair. "What's going on here?"

"Isn't he just the most devious character?" Mrs. Peifer cooed, relinquishing her hold on his hand. "He came up with the idea."

Lyssa could feel her blood pressure spike. Devious and then some.

As though reading her mind, Mrs. Peifer continued, "He really is going to sell this place. His wife, well, ex-wife really, she was the one who wanted something sprawling and impressive. He only bought it to please her." She gave an unladylike snort. "And then she had the nerve to insist on his chalet in Vail instead when they split. And Robert's been too busy to unload it. Until now. And really, Ms. Markham, I do want to see that Ashleigh Lane home. Our place is simply too big now that all the children are married. We're going to sell it to our oldest son and take back a mortgage. I'd like to be in a smaller home before Christmas."

She came to stand next to Lyssa. "And I want you to find us our new home. You were so patient on the phone this afternoon, I just knew you were the kind of person I wanted to work with. And Robert, well, he said he had met you and wanted to invite you to dinner. To me it was a no-brainer, to combine dinner with inspecting this house to list it. I was happy to bring you here. And I don't mind you showing me the house tomorrow."

Taking a deep breath while trying to assimilate this unexpected turn of events, Lyssa said neutrally, "I see."

Savidge stepped toward her. "It's all up to you, of course. You can leave with Charlene now and show her the house she mentioned, or do it tomorrow. Or I can walk you through this museum today and we can sign a listing agreement. And if you can, I'd love to have you stay for dinner. Yuki is a marvelous chef and he's famous for his boeuf bourguignon."

"And chocolate mousse," Mrs. Peifer added.

Yuki, standing to one side of the kitchen waiting patiently to return to the range, inclined his dark head in acknowledgement.

"I think," Lyssa said carefully, "I should take Mrs. Peifer to see the house. The owners are expecting us and it would be discourteous not to show up. Selling a house is traumatic enough when things go well."

"Of course you're right, dear. See, Robert—" she turned to him, "—that's one of the reasons I wanted her to handle your sale. She has such a nice manner about her."

Savidge's smile turned downright devilish as he said, "Nice. Yes. Very nice."

Lyssa felt her cheeks heat at his intense look. She spun on her heel and gestured to Mrs. Peifer. "That's settled, then. Let's go."

"And in, let's say an hour, Robert can come pick you up." Mrs. Peifer nodded her head decisively and strode down the hallway toward the front door, leaving Lyssa standing openmouthed.

"I'll be there," he said, eyes twinkling. "Now that Charlene started the ball rolling, I can't wait to unload this monster."

Trapped. If she asked Mrs. Peifer to chauffeur her back to the office to pick up her car, she might alienate her and lose a sale. And turning down the listing on a three-million-dollar dwelling on the most prestigious street on the Main Line wasn't an option. She'd be a fool to walk away from a one-percent listing commission regardless of who sold the house. As to the dinner invitation, she'd deal with that when the time came. After he signed the listing agreement. She was a working gal, she reminded herself sternly.

"Fine." She followed Mrs. Peifer down the hall, only to hear Savidge's footsteps right behind her. Of course he'd be gracious enough to say goodbye to his friend, she thought.

At the door, Mrs. Peifer turned to face her friend, a puckish smile on her face. "By the way, you didn't happen to send anyone flowers today, did you?"

"Guilty."

"Aha, I thought so. When I walked into the real estate office, the scent of all those red roses was positively transporting! What a romantic gesture!"

Lyssa cleared her throat. "Yes, I've, uh, been meaning to thank you for them. It was a little...overwhelming."

"Overdone?" Savidge's mouth quirked up on one side. "Showing off?"

"Oh, don't pay any attention to him, dear," Mrs. Peifer said. "He does this kind of thing all the time. He just loves to give things to people. Why, I remember when he bought my Jack an electric golf cart because he said he'd always wanted one but never got around to ordering it."

"Don't go giving away all my secrets, Charlene, or I'll have to take back that bush you love so much."

"No you don't, young man, you dig up my Harry Lauder's Walking Stick and I'll crack you over the head with a golf club."

Lyssa stood watching in astonishment at the relaxed byplay. Here was a totally different facet of the sexual master, the no-holds-barred attorney, the friend who helped her stand up to her ex. Next thing, she'd probably find out he owned a Lhasa apso or some other tiny lapdog.

"Well, let's not keep Ashleigh Lane waiting," Mrs. Peifer said. And out the door she went.

Slightly dazed at having been manipulated so expertly, Lyssa followed her into the Lexus. In a few moments they were back at the Tudor and Lyssa was making introductions all around. The home was charming, well laid out and nicely upgraded, and Mrs. Peifer made noises about bringing her husband around next week, after he returned from his golf tournament in southern California.

At the door, everyone shook hands. Lyssa felt a sale was a real possibility, and her spirits rose. As the two women descended the steps, a sleek, shimmery, blue two-seater pulled up behind Mrs. Peifer's Lexus. It wasn't until it was close enough to read the logo that Lyssa saw it was an Aston Martin. Involuntarily she licked her lips. It was classic, understated, elegant, and she fell in love with it instantly.

Then Savidge opened the door and got out. Her mouth went dry.

And she knew what her decision would be.

Chapter Eight

"If you'll just sign both copies right here..."

Savidge bent forward and scrawled his name on the listing agreement. Lyssa curbed the urge to shoot her fist in the air and yell, "Yessss!" She would arrange to have the twenty-room home professionally appraised in the next week to ensure an accurate listing price, but she was certain it would be close to her original estimate of three million dollars. Even sharing the one percent listing fee with the agency would net her enough to prepay several months of her mortgage.

When it sold.

"It's a stunning showpiece," she said as she signed both copies and handed him one. Six bedrooms and four baths comprised the second floor, with a six-room in-law apartment on the third floor, which at one time had been servants' quarters. All the moldings were cherry with a fine patina, closets plentiful, the baths modern.

Savidge shook his head ruefully, his glance bouncing around the very masculine study off the living room. A full wall of books, comfortable leather sofa and club chairs in rich burgundy, three state-of-the-art computers on a cherry-wood slab of a desk made the spacious room seem cozy. "I certainly held onto this white elephant long enough. I was too busy to move, so I just transferred my bedroom downstairs. I do love that kitchen, though." His eyes twinkled. "You'll have to find me another home that has a chef's kitchen, or Yuki will quit on me."

"You don't cook at all?" Lyssa folded her copy of the agreement and slipped it into her satchel, trying not to count dollar signs in the carrot he was obliquely offering her.

"I dabble. When I have the time. Whenever I return from a transcontinental trip, I bless Yuki and his skill. The freezer's always full of heat-and-eat, gourmet style."

"I couldn't tell which was his room. All the upstairs bedrooms seem, well, feminine."

"That's my ex's doing. She's the one who hired the decorator. But Yuki only stays over when I ask. He's kind of a jack-of-all-trades for me."

"Oh."

The conversation dwindled. Lyssa couldn't think of anything else to say. She should ask him to drive her back to her car, still parked at the office. She should ask if his invitation to stay for dinner was still open. She wondered if he would kiss her senseless.

She wondered if she was losing her mind.

Savidge cleared his throat. "Lyssa, I—"

Lyssa held her breath, keeping her eyes downcast.

"Look at me."

Slowly she lifted her lashes. And saw a mixture of emotions crossing his face. Lust, chagrin, little-boy shyness…anxiety?

"We didn't exactly meet in a traditional way," he began.

Lyssa stiffened.

He raked a hand through his thick hair. "What I mean to say is, we've never had a traditional date. You know, a movie, dancing, whatever it is that couples do when they're getting to know each other." He gave her one of those rueful, Harrison Ford smiles that set her knees to trembling. "I've been out of the dating game for so long, I just—"

He paced the floor of the study. "I don't mean to sound conceited, but I'm accustomed to women throwing themselves at me. I never lacked for arm candy or a willing—" He cleared his throat again.

"Hell. What I'm trying to say is, would you like to share Yuki's dinner creation with me tonight? And maybe we'll go out dancing afterwards?"

Touched, Lyssa said, "I'd love to have dinner with you." She looked down at her no-nonsense business suit with its sheath skirt. "Not sure about the dancing, though."

An enigmatic, Cheshire cat smile appeared on his face. "We'll talk about it later."

With that, he gave her his arm and walked her to the nook adjoining the kitchen. "I hope you don't mind, I thought this would be more comfortable than that huge table in the dining room." He gave a mock shudder. "I hated all those formal dinners Columba insisted on having. Did you know the table opens up to seat twenty-four? And there's two, count 'em, two sets of china, both of them horrendously expensive, for each seat. Why she didn't take that crap with her..." He shook his head as if in disbelief.

"What a yard sale they'd make," Lyssa teased.

Chuckling, he handed her into a well-padded banquette covered in cheery yellow chintz. The butcher-block table was set for two with tableware in muted earth tones on green woven mats. Sunflowers bloomed in a copper pitcher alongside a wine cooler filled with a dark brown bottle nestled in cracked ice.

Picking up a red-and-white-checked towel, Savidge grasped the bottle and began working the cork. "You like champagne? I thought we'd toast our new business arrangement. For starters."

The *pop* was audible. He poured the bubbling liquid into two waiting flutes and settled the bottle back into its bed of ice, picked up both glasses, and handed her one.

"To the future," he said.

Lyssa's heart did a little flip-flop. "The future."

They sipped. "Now. You just sit there. Yuki did the hard part, and now he's gone home. All I have to do is put water on for the noodles." He lifted the lid of the *boeuf* and inhaled. "Ahhh. *Perfectamento.* I hope you're hungry."

"Smells wonderful." Her stomach growled.

He laughed. Their eyes met. "Good. I am, too."

Laughing with him, she watched as Savidge worked in the kitchen with no wasted motion, graceful as a ballet dancer. He added curly noodles to boiling water, tossed a mesclun salad with a balsamic vinaigrette and spooned portions into wooden bowls. In due course, he set a steaming plate in front of her, chunks of beef tenderloin slow-simmered in rich red wine sauce, pearl onions and sliced mushrooms, lying on a bed of noodles, with stir-fried snap peas on the side.

Between sips of champagne, they nibbled on the food and haltingly explored each other's psyches. They discovered a mutual love of classic movies, discussed the merits of Ted Turner's colorized versions versus the original black and white, whether *Citizen Kane* was better than *Casablanca*. They laughed at the excesses of Busby

Berkley-style revues and the intricacy of Esther Williams' water ballets. She told him of her trek to New Hampshire to settle Michelle at Dartmouth. He told her of his twenty-one-year-old son taking a semester at Cambridge, England to study Shakespeare. She discovered he enjoyed golf, sailing, chess and jazz. She told him she liked gardening, reading, biking and classical music.

All too soon the champagne and the light outside the bow window were gone, and only remnants of the meal remained on their plates.

"Ready for dessert?"

Lyssa massaged her stomach. "Everything was so good, I pigged out on seconds. I couldn't eat another bite. Honest."

"Well, then," he said with a sly look, "we'll have to kill some time until there's room for dessert." He reached a hand out to her. "Come with me."

Suddenly shy, Lyssa had a difficult time getting to her feet. He'd been vivacious and charming during dinner, with not a hint of the sexual innuendo or lust that he'd exhibited in the past. She liked this new Robert Savidge; she would have no qualms introducing this side of him to her daughter. But she could feel heat building inside her at the prospect of his naked body hard against hers, plunging into her until she cried out in passion.

He led her to his bedroom off the study, with its massive four-poster bed that could have been taken from a British duke's ancestral home. She had just glimpsed the room when they were taking inventory for the listing earlier. Now she could see the room had the same masculine feel as the study, unlike all the upstairs rooms. Enlarged photographs of a nineteenth-century sailing vessel — with him as a crew member, he told her — graced the dark green walls. Two carved antique armoires flanked a twelve-foot-high pier mirror.

With a hand at the small of her back, Savidge nudged her beyond the bed and into a bathroom as big as her living room. She stopped just inside the doorway and looked at him quizzically.

"We're going dancing, remember? I thought you'd like to freshen up first."

He opened a door to a small closet. "I think you'll find everything you need in here."

"How in the world...?" Her voice trailed off as she spied a padded hanger holding her favorite party dress, a black cap-sleeve A-line that skimmed her knees and displayed a hint of cleavage in the scoop neck.

"Kat," he said succinctly.

"That little sneak." But Lyssa couldn't put much oomph into the epithet. She was too overwhelmed by the thought behind the action. On both their parts.

"Think you could be ready by — " he checked his gold Patek Philippe " — nine- thirty? I have a table reserved for ten p.m. in downtown Philadelphia."

Lyssa glanced at her own no-name watch. An hour. She swallowed.

"I'll be on the computer in the study. If you need anything, soap, towels, back rub, just sing out."

And he was gone, the door closing softly behind him.

I wonder if my mouth is hanging open, she thought. Then she spied her overnight bag on the floor of the closet. Knowing Kat, it held a change of underwear and her makeup kit.

She let herself sink onto the padded bench at the dressing table and stared at her reflection in a mirror lit with strips of bright lights on both sides. *Back rub?*

A smile played around the edges of her mouth. What if she filled the tub with bubbles and hot water and, as he put it, sang out for a back rub and see where that led?

But oh, what would it feel like to be in his arms on a café dance floor, swaying slowly to a smoky contralto singing vintage Sinatra? To have a real date? With a really, really, *really* virile man? Could they pull this off without a detour to fuck like rabbits? Or would the dancing be more foreplay, with the delicious addition of anticipation spiced by the agony of waiting?

With a decisive nod, she reached for her bag.

* * * * *

Humming as she put the hot rollers to her hair, Lyssa reviewed the strategy she'd formulated while taking a quick shower. Her eyes sparkled with several coats of mascara and a touch of dark shadow. The sheer demi-bra and thong she'd never worn before made her feel extra sexy. *Thank you, Kat, for making me buy them!* She wondered how long she'd be able to dance in those strappy, high-heeled sandals Kat had packed, then decided she could always lean into her partner if she got tired.

She removed the rollers, combed and arranged her hair, then put her plan into action.

"Savidge?" she called out. "Can you help me?"

When he strolled into the bathroom, she had posed herself with her front facing the door, her head turned to look over her shoulder at the mirror as though trying to get a glimpse of her back. She knew he'd get hit with both barrels, seeing both sides of her at once in her Victoria's Secret unmentionables, her breasts lifted and thrust forward above the underwire, her ass cheeks in the mirror emphasized by the sliver of fire-engine-red nylon separating them.

She allowed her gaze to meet his reflected one. "I seem to have gotten a bite or something, and I can't reach it. It kind of burns and itches. Can you take a look?"

"I'm looking, I'm looking," he rasped. But he stood statue-still. He had changed into a white shirt and dark tie and looked good enough to tackle right then and there.

Because he still hadn't moved, she sauntered to him, feeling positively decadent in her heels and skimpy underwear and swaying hips. His gaze burned into her, touching her nipples to make them tighten into hard buds, then raking down her belly to her crotch, where liquid heat pooled deep within her.

Slowly she turned, lifting her curls off her shoulder, bending her head forward. "Somewhere down my back," she said. "See if you can find a red mark."

He put warm—very warm—hands on her shoulders and gently nudged her closer to the mirror. "Where the light's better," he growled. He trailed the fingertips of both hands from her nape and down her spine to the top of her thong, then back up again, head bent forward until she could feel the heat of his breath on her skin.

"Can't feel anything," he murmured. "Turn around."

He positioned her so her profile was reflected in the mirror then stood behind her, the lights casting soft shadows on every indentation of her vertebrae. His lips followed the trail his fingers had taken. Occasionally he stopped to lick a spot then said, "Nope, that isn't it."

Transfixed, and utterly turned on by the stark difference in their attire, Lyssa watched in the mirror as Savidge licked, nuzzled, touched and nibbled his way up and down her back, still denying he could see the spot she'd asked him to find, and keeping his hands to himself, damn his eyes! He scooped a bottle from the dressing table, pushed the plunger to release a dab of lotion. Setting the bottle down, he rubbed his palms together, then slowly, sensually, massaged the lotion into the skin between the straps of her bra, then underneath the back strip, and down to her waist.

Unable to resist, she turned, placing her aching breasts in the path of his palms. She wanted, no, *needed* his mouth suckling on her nipples *right this minute*.

He backed away, sat down abruptly on the makeup bench. "It's almost nine-thirty." It came out a little breathless. "Do you need help getting your dress on?"

Her eyes widened. Okaaaay, two could play this game.

She stepped up to him, hands on his shoulders, then spread her legs and sat down on him, lap-dance fashion.

"I might." She wiggled around until her crotch seated itself right astride his hard-on then pillowed her breasts against his chest as she started kissing his jaw, his neck, his earlobe. The heat from his cock flowed through his trousers and up into her spread legs. She pressed down on the throbbing length of it, clenched her thighs together to squeeze his hips. His sharp intake of breath made her smile.

"Come to think of it," she murmured as she slid off his lap, "I can handle it." Hips swaying, she strolled to the closet, lifted the silky black dress off its hanger, and slipped it over her head. Turning to the mirror, she adjusted the lay of the sleeves, settled the darts for maximum enhancement of her breasts, then leaned forward—exposing a nice bit of cleavage, if she did say so herself—and applied a bit of lip gloss on her slightly swollen lips.

A spritz of Shalimar, then, "I'm ready."

Savidge hadn't moved from the bench.

* * * * *

As they entered the basement club on Samson Street in old-town Philadelphia, a wailing sax trilled a counterpoint to a mocha-skinned woman making verbal love to the microphone in a sultry alto voice. The small jazz club was everything Lyssa imagined it might be. Tiny tables crowded around a small stage that also accommodated a young woman at an upright piano, bassist, and a drummer who right now was dreamily swishing wire brushes across the drumhead. After paying the cover and slipping the host something extra, Savidge escorted her to their reserved table along a wall, close enough to see without being blasted by the music, far enough from the bar to be out of the way, and within two tables of the postage-stamp dance floor.

They ordered—a Guinness for him, a Kir for her—then settled down to enjoy the ambiance and the music. The noise level wasn't loud enough to inhibit conversation, but somehow, words felt superfluous here. Lyssa found herself humming, and sometimes singing snatches of songs with the group. Their drinks arrived, they touched glasses in a silent toast, and listened while they sipped. The bluesy number was followed by an upbeat jazz number. Then the chanteuse left the stage and the combo slipped into a slow, dreamy rendition of "Smoke Gets in Your Eyes".

Savidge stood. "Dance?"

The steamy look in his eyes sent shivers up and down Lyssa's spine. She placed her hand in his outstretched one and followed him to the crowded floor. His right arm encircled her, palm resting on her bare back. He tucked her head into the crook of his neck. His left hand cradled hers close to his heart. She heard the deep hum of his voice as he murmured a few words of the song here and there.

Lyssa closed her eyes in sheer bliss and allowed her other senses to take over. The heat emanating from him, chest to thighs pressed against her. His steady heartbeat beneath her hand. The scent of smoke and alcohol and warm bodies. Her Shalimar and his elusive male scent. The timeless music, with grace notes and riffs from the pianist in counterpoint to the low beat of the bass. She wanted to raise her head to taste the salt on his skin, the tang of Guinness on his tongue.

Disappointment lanced through her when the music ended. Savidge bent down to whisper in her ear. "The ladies' room is right beyond that door. I want you to go in there and take those red panties off."

Lyssa's eyes popped open. She pushed against his hold so she could look into his eyes. They looked positively black in the low light, with only a tiny glow from the stage lights reflecting off them. "Wh-what did you say?"

"Take them off. I want to know you're sitting right next to me, or dancing right up against me, wearing nothing underneath but that tantalizing perfume." He emphasized his request by walking her to the ladies' room door. "I'll wait for you."

"But where will I put it? My purse is back at the…"

His smile was devastatingly seductive. "That tiny string you're wearing will fit in my pants pocket and no one will ever suspect."

Lyssa let her eyes drop to his mouth. It had softened with desire. His tongue flicked over his lower lip, making her breath come out in short gasps. Her skin tingled all over. Could she? Did she dare? Who would know? What would George say?

That thought was enough to put some starch in her spine. She lifted onto tiptoe and gave Savidge's lower lip, the damp one he'd just licked, a quick nibble then turned to the ladies' room.

A few moments later, nervous and excited all at once, she opened the door a crack and peeked out. The look he gave her was dark, earthy. Lustful. His hand reached out and she thrust the scrap of red silk into it. Nonchalantly he slipped both hand and silk into his trousers pocket, then walked her back onto the dance floor, snuggling her right back into his arms even closer than before.

"Imagination is funny…" he sang along with the chanteuse, who had returned to the stage. He murmured more words, like "bee" and "honey", but all she could think of was the honey that was already pooling in her crotch from the most erotic thing she had ever done.

The dance floor was even more crowded now, and she felt Savidge's hand slide down lower on her back, then lower still to cup one of her ass cheeks and press her closer and yet closer to him. Her four-inch heels raised her high enough that she could almost feel his cock between her legs, but not quite enough, not nearly enough. She wanted him to hoist her up with his large hands under her butt so she could wrap her legs around him. A shudder zapped through her. Oh God, this was torture. Pure, unadulterated, sweet torture, to be so close to him, to know the heights of ecstasy to which they could soar together, and not be able to get any closer. She wanted to leave right this minute, wanted to rush home with him and fuck him right on the floor of her foyer, no, right in the bucket seats of his Aston Martin. She trembled with the need of it.

"Cold?" he murmured.

"No," she managed to gasp. "Too damn hot."

His low chuckle reverberated to every nerve ending she possessed. He took his left hand from hers, leaving her palm against his heart, and stroked up and down her bare arm, then onto her bare back, trapping her even closer until she wondered if a strip of dental floss could fit between them. His right hand still clasped her ass. He rubbed his palm up and down across the silky black fabric, and she wondered briefly if he was trying to lift her skirt to show the other patrons what she was—wasn't—wearing underneath.

"Don't you dare," she murmured.

"Dare what?"

Lyssa decided discretion was better than giving him ideas. "Nothing."

Cheek to cheek, she could feel his mouth stretch into a smile. "I would dare," he whispered, "but I want you all to myself tonight."

Her lashes fluttered down. *Me, too*, she thought.

The music stopped. They clung to each other, still swaying from the echoes and images inside their brains, as other dancers moved past them. Reluctantly Lyssa pulled away from Savidge a millimeter or two. Their eyes met.

"Let's split," he rasped.

* * * * *

"Wake up, sleepyhead."

Interrupted from a delicious dream of Savidge licking her inner thighs, Lyssa jolted awake. Blinking, she looked around. And saw the burled wood and leather interior of a luxurious automobile. The Aston Martin. Parked in her driveway, headlights and engine off.

Oh God, had she fallen asleep on the way home?

Her face flamed in embarrassment. How could she have committed such a faux pas? What kind of signal had she given the urbane, sophisticated, sexy Robert Savidge? That she was a country hick who couldn't stay awake past midnight? Or maybe he thought she couldn't hold her liquor? She'd only had the one Kir at the club, and a couple of glasses of champagne several hours prior.

Before she could apologize, he was out of the car and opening her door. "Why don't you find your keys before you get out?" he suggested with aplomb.

She did, fumbling in her purse, and handed the key ring to him, then swung her legs around and allowed him to help her out, as she wasn't sure of her ability to stand unaided. Wrapping an arm around her waist, he walked her up the steps to the front porch.

"Which is the key to your car?"

Lyssa blinked again. "My car?"

"I'll have Yuki deliver it first thing tomorrow. Is eight o'clock good for you?"

Her car. Her car was still parked in front of the office. Oh God, what would Evann and Bernadette say? She managed to shift her brain into thinking gear and pointed out the Honda key. Eight o'clock? Would Savidge still be here? "Eight is fine," she stammered.

He swiftly removed and pocketed the car key then found the house key and inserted it. He nudged the door open a crack and slipped the key ring back into her purse.

"Come here," he rasped.

In an instant he had her pressed against the doorjamb, his mouth ravaging hers. She opened her mouth to his insistent tongue, both of them giving, welcoming, demanding. A groan sounded deep within him, and she answered it with a sigh of her own as she wiggled her body in an effort to get closer and closer still to his heat, to the heavy bulge straining against his trousers. His hands slid up and down her sides, thumbs skimming her breasts. He moved his mouth to her neck and took savage nips. Any thought of drowsiness fled from Lyssa's brain, replaced with wondering why they stood on the porch making out like teenagers instead of stepping inside and ripping each other's clothes off.

"God, what you do to me." Savidge's voice was shaky, his breaths uneven and harsh in her ear.

She felt his hands grip her upper arms, as if undecided whether to thrust her aside or pull her into him. He tipped his head, resting his forehead on hers, and breathed her name.

Trembling with need, Lyssa strained to bring their bodies together again, but his hands were like iron pincers, keeping them no more than a foot apart. He took a deep breath, spoke her name again. She lifted her head to meet his intense gaze, his pupils dilated until no color showed in his irises.

"I'm leaving for London in a couple of hours," he finally said. "I'll call you tomorrow night." With that, he spun her around, pushed the front door open for her, and nudged her across the threshold. "Sleep well."

And he was gone.

Feeling betrayed and abandoned, Lyssa stood in the doorway and watched until the red taillights of the Aston Martin disappeared into the foggy darkness.

Chapter Nine

"I don't understand. Why all the secrecy?" Frowning, Lyssa stared at the black silk scarf in her friend's hand.

Kat shrugged. "Rules."

"Rules for what?"

With what Lyssa could only characterize as a devilish look, Kat said, "You either trust me or you don't, Lyss. I'm not going to throw you to the lions at the Roman Coliseum."

An image of Savidge in his gladiator costume sprang full-blown on the screen of Lyssa's mind. *Nah*, she thought. Her friend wasn't aiding and abetting him for nefarious purposes. Besides, Savidge was in London, damn it. When he'd walked away from the front door the previous evening, she'd been so bewitched, she hadn't even called out to stop him. She'd had to concentrate on keeping her knees from buckling at the torrid goodnight kiss he'd given her after all that first-class foreplay on the dance floor.

She'd spent the remainder of the night in restless sleep, bewildered at this change in his attitude. Almost as though he wanted them to have a normal dating relationship.

Normal. That kiss was anything but normal.

Her lips had been singed from his heat.

And he'd left her aching for him, thinking of him, daydreaming at the real estate office all day long until the clock dragged its hands to six and she could punch out.

Thank God Kat had diverted her attention by inviting her to an "intimate get-together" at her house. At least that's what she'd said. Now here they were, standing in Kat's foyer, her friend dangling the black silk from her hands.

"It's just a routine precaution," Kat insisted. "You know, you're going to have to work on this trust issue. I'm not George."

Damn, but Kat knew just which buttons to push. She would do anything that was the antithesis of her scrungy ex. "Give me the blindfold."

"I'll do it. Turn around."

Giving her a gimlet stare, Lyssa said, "You don't trust me to cover my eyes all the way?"

"I just want to be sure your hair doesn't get mussed."

With a hmmmph, Lyssa allowed herself to be blindfolded and led onto Kat's porch, down the steps, and into the passenger seat of a car. The faint scent of Kat's Obsession and the rich smell of new leather told her that it was Kat's BMW. She fumbled with the seat belt, heard the driver's door open, then close.

"All set?" Kat's chipper voice.

"You're really testing our friendship, lady."

With an evil chuckle, Kat turned the ignition, and the car sprang into action.

Behind the blindfold, Lyssa closed her eyes and concentrated on following the car's movement. A few blocks on Windermere Drive, then a right, then a left. The car accelerated. The car stopped. Lyssa tensed. Then it moved forward again. *Traffic light.* They must be on Lancaster Avenue, she thought. Soon Lyssa lost all sense of direction. How long had they driven? Ten minutes? A half hour? Had that long curve been to get onto the Blue Route? Had Kat been making devious turns to confuse her? Which, as Kat well knew, couldn't be too hard. George had always denigrated her navigation skills whenever they'd driven anywhere together.

"Okay, we're here."

Adrenaline pumped through Lyssa. What did Kat have planned? She knew darn well she could trust her best friend, but still, everything was so secretive that Lyssa's equilibrium was disrupted.

The door on the passenger side opened before Kat got out of the car. A large hand took a firm grip on Lyssa's shoulder. "Easy, now," a deep male voice said. "Just swing your legs out. I'll guide you."

"Thank you, Jules." Kat's voice, right next to him.

"You're coming with me, aren't you, Kat?" Lyssa spoke with just a hint of panic.

"Wouldn't miss it."

That didn't help Lyssa's unease.

With Kat on her left and Jules on her right, Lyssa was led down an echoing hallway. No steps. They must have pulled inside a garage. They stopped a moment then she was nudged forward again. Four steps and they stopped. A soft hum, a whir.

Her stomach lurched.

An elevator. An office building? Hotel? She hadn't been in the real estate business long, but she hadn't heard of a *house* that had an elevator.

A whoosh and the elevator doors slid open. They had gone up quite a few floors, twenty or more. Definitely not a house. Deep carpeting underfoot as she walked. The click of a latch—a door opening. Lyssa detected perfume mingled with masculine cologne, heard the clink of ice cubes in a glass, the murmur of voices. A shiver raced up her spine.

"Steady," Kat whispered. Then, in a louder voice, "Stand right here. The formalities will only take a few minutes."

A deep, authoritative male voice said, "You have been nominated for membership in the Platinum Society. As you already know, it's an exclusive bastion of Main Line Philadelphians with rigid requirements. You are in the presence of the board of directors, who vote on prospective new members. If you are accepted for membership, you will, of course, be afforded the answers to any questions you have, including identities."

The sex club. *Of course. They don't want outsiders to know their secrets.* Lyssa relaxed marginally, then tensed with the thought, *Who nominated me? Kat? Savidge?*

"Could you please tell us what you thought of the masquerade you attended in late August?" A female voice, not Kat's. Throaty, with a Katharine Hepburn diction.

Lyssa felt her cheeks heat. Had this board of directors seen her wanton behavior? She stalled, wondering what they wanted to hear.

"Please be frank with us," Kat said. "No one will bite you."

"Unless you request it," another male voice said to a few chuckles.

"I, uh, I was amazed to see...everything that was happening," she stuttered.

"That's a normal reaction," the Hepburn clone said. "But can you tell us how you felt when you watched the guests interacting?"

Now her face had to be lipstick-red, Lyssa thought. She could feel a bead of sweat trickle down between her breasts just from the heat of remembering the Indian, the fireman, the Scotsman...her gladiator. "Turned on," she managed. Then her voice strengthened. She wasn't George's doormat any more. She was a woman who had discovered her own sensuality and was delighted and rocked by it.

"I never realized that I could...that just watching could turn me on. I-I hate pornographic movies, because it's all about the man putting part A into slot B, then slot C, then slot D, and so on, and so forth. But this was different. The participants, they weren't acting for the benefit of a camera or a paycheck. They were *enjoying* themselves."

She took a deep breath, wishing she had changed from her office suit into more casual, less constricting clothes. The jabot at her neck was particularly smothering.

"I enjoyed watching them. I, uh, I got into the spirit of things." She resisted the urge to raise her hands to feel just how hot her cheeks were. It would just call attention to the furious blush that was spreading down to her throat.

"How would you feel if I asked you to take all your clothes off right now?" This from the man Kat had called Jules, who had met them at the car.

Lyssa swallowed. "I'm not sure. If I'm the only one, I think it would be uncomfortable. Especially with the blindfold on and not knowing where I am."

"You can invite us to disrobe at any time," the authoritative voice said. He must be the chairman of the board.

"For all you know, we're already naked," the other male said. "Would you like me to rub my body against yours so you can discover for yourself?"

"I think I'll pass, thanks."

"Is my presence restraining your response in any way?" Kat asked. "Because I can leave if I make you feel uncomfortable."

"Oh God, no, Kat, don't leave. I-I really would like to have a friend here."

"We're all friends," the chairman said. "The members have all seen each other naked. We're comfortable with our bodies, our desires. We're comfortable with each other. You saw firsthand how men backed off as soon as you said the word. There is absolutely no intimidation in this group, Lyssa. That's why we go through such a rigid screening process."

Lyssa knew a moment of panic when he called her by name. But then she chastised herself. Of course he knew her name, first and last. After all, someone had nominated her for membership. Also, she obviously had to have been approved simply to attend the masquerade.

The chairman spoke again. "You have received recommendations from several of our members. You were observed at the gathering and your behavior was considered acceptable. If we here today approve you for membership, you will have to read and agree to our bylaws. That includes not divulging the names of any members to anyone. Not even to your lawyer or doctor."

"I-I certainly can hold confidences," Lyssa volunteered.

"Good. You should also know," the chairman said, "that you cannot *ask* to join. Oh, sure, you can browbeat a member to put your name for nomination, if you are able to discover who any of the members are. But you cannot worm your way into our group unless a formal nomination is made by a member in good standing and voted on unanimously by the board."

She didn't know what to say to that, so she said nothing.

"We'll just take a few minutes for our deliberations. Why don't you sit down?" The man called Jules was at her side, guiding her to a nearby chair. She sat and waited, her mind racing. She hadn't even considered becoming a member. Did she want to be? How much were dues or initiation fees? Was it fair to ask her to accept the conditions *before* she read the bylaws? Did she want to share Savidge with other women? Did she want Kat to know how wanton she was?

Well, *that* was silly. Kat already knew. She had seen it in her before Lyssa herself had. She should be thanking Kat for awakening her long-dormant sensuality, thank her for bringing her into contact with Savidge. As to sharing him, heck, had they made any promises? Any commitments? Sure, Savidge was any woman's wet dream, but even before she'd seen him, the other men had revved her juices to a mind-blowing pitch.

Why, even just looking had turned her on. So, yeah, she wanted to be a member. If Savidge would turn out to be only a flash in the pan, she would still have her sensuality, her hunger, and an outlet for it. Any number of outlets, actually.

Her body hummed at the thought. Lyssa Markham, sex goddess. George would have a shit-fit. But then, she guessed she wouldn't be able to tell him.

No matter. She'd made her decision.

"Lyssa?" Jules took her hand, helped her rise.

"The board has voted you into membership," the chairman said. "If you choose to decline, this offer will not be extended again, nor will you be invited to another function. If you accept, we will require a notarized oath that you will not divulge any information, including but not limited to, the identity of any member."

An absurd feeling of relief claimed Lyssa. Had she been worried she'd be found wanting?

"How say you?"

She cleared her throat. "I accept the offer to become a member."

There was a general murmur of pleasure. Lyssa felt hands moving at the back of her head. The blindfold fell to her shoulders.

She blinked. She was standing in a spacious living room subtly lit with table lamps near several sofa groupings. The skyline of center city Philadelphia twinkled through a wall of windows. They might be in the Ritz Carlton Hotel, she thought, judging by her view of the twin peaks of One and Two Liberty Place. Or maybe one of the other four-star hotels. And in the penthouse, if her perspective was correct.

She lowered her eyes to the long table in front of her. Arrayed like the tribunal of judges that they were, sat a handsome, older, white-haired man with piercing whiskey-colored eyes and massive jaw; a man about Lyssa's age with a receding hairline, sensual lips, and fashionable wire-rimmed glasses; and a stunning, red-haired woman whose face seemed familiar. The man who had removed her blindfold, Jules, and Kat completed the board. All were fully clothed, in what Lyssa thought looked like hand-tailored suits on the men and a haute couture dress on the woman. Truly the cream of upper-class Philadelphia.

"It's time to open the champagne," the white-haired man declared, his voice that of what she thought of as the chairman. He rose, came around the table to Lyssa, and took her face in both of his large hands. "Welcome to the Platinum Society." He kissed her, softly at first, rocking his face to graze her mouth with his, then more forcefully, nudging her lips apart with a tongue as fiery as a chili pepper. Getting into the spirit of the event, she leaned into him, softening her mouth to cling to his. The man knew how to kiss. She reveled in the sheer delight of it, nothing but their mouths touching, and his hands on her cheeks.

"Wow," she said when they finally pulled apart.

With a devastating smile, he reached inside his jacket and withdrew a hinged bracelet, no more than a quarter-inch wide, inscribed with an intricate design Lyssa couldn't decipher without a jeweler's loupe. Taking her right hand, he affixed it to her wrist and closed the clasp. "This is our secret handshake, if you will. Any member can recognize any other member by this trinket. It's made of platinum, like our name." He pulled his cuff back over his right forearm to display his own. "See?"

A frown formed on Lyssa's brow. "But I thought all the members know each other?"

"Ah, here in suburban Philadelphia, we do. But there are several chapters in European capitals. This assures club entrée to a member in another location."

"Champagne?" Jules interrupted, handing each of them a flute of bubbly.

"To Lyssa Markham, our newest member." The chairman touched his glass to hers. The others crowded around, clinking glasses. He introduced Lyssa to the redhead, who, she realized, was the belly dancer at the masquerade, and to the other man.

With a wicked gleam in his eye, he continued, "And I'm Peyton Savidge. Robert's father."

* * * * *

"I thought I'd die when he told me his name," Lyssa said to Kat as they entered Lyssa's kitchen for a postmortem. "All I could think of was, I screwed your son." She tossed her suit jacket onto a kitchen chair and ran water into the Braun coffeemaker. "Decaf okay?"

"Fine. You know," Kat said casually, "Peyton was there that night. After all, it was his house. I'm sure he saw you seducing his son with that scorching dance you did."

Lyssa plugged in the coffeepot, then turned slowly to face her friend. "I have to say, I'm ambivalent about my membership. Maybe I said yes because I knew I wouldn't be invited again, and I didn't want to close any doors. After all, I don't *have* to participate in anything, I don't *have* to attend the next masquerade or picnic or dance."

"If it makes you feel any better, I felt the same way when I joined. Now, I take my sexuality for granted."

"And it shows," Lyssa admitted. "You have a—I don't know—a kind of self-assurance, a certain way you hold your head up, that comes from loving yourself, loving your body. I could use a little more self-confidence."

"Honey, I can tell you that the entire board was hoping you'd take them up on the request to take your clothes off. You have the lush look of an odalisque, a Marilyn Monroe kind of body that today's skinny movie stars can't hope to match. Your self-confidence is already surfacing since that turd dropped out of your life."

An involuntary shudder rippled through Lyssa at the reference to her ex. "I wonder if he told his *bride* what happened at your poolside." The memory of Savidge playing along to thumb their collective noses at George made her grin. She glanced at the digital clock atop the wall oven. Nine o'clock. It was two in the morning in London. She wondered if Savidge was sleeping.

Another, darker thought made her purse her lips. Was there a London Platinum Society? Was he even now enjoying someone else's dance of seduction?

So what? They had no ties, no commitment. None whatsoever. He probably had mind-blowing sex with all his partners.

Trying to derail that distasteful train of thought, she said, "Want a brownie? I have some in the freezer." Without waiting for a response, she pulled out two of the chewy chocolate confections and popped them into the microwave to thaw, then filled two mugs with fresh brew.

Just then the doorbell rang. Lyssa's heart skipped a beat.

Savidge. Had he flown home already?

Of course not. He had business in London. It hadn't even been twenty-four hours since he'd left U.S. soil.

Lyssa and Kat exchanged glances. Lyssa shrugged an *I don't know who it is* gesture. Taking her mug with her, she moved to the front door, and peered through the peephole.

"George," she muttered. "What the heck does he want at this time of night?"

For a moment she was tempted to just let him stand there until he got tired of leaning on the bell. But he'd obviously seen Kat's car in the driveway, seen the lights on, and knew they were still up. It would be just like him to keep ringing until his finger fell off.

Resigned, she unlatched the safety chain, turned the deadbolt and opened the door.

"It took you long enough. What the devil were you doing?"

"And good evening to you, too, George. Are you going to come in or are you just going to stand there glowering at me?"

With a scowl, her ex stalked into the hallway, giving her clingy silk shell the once-over, noting her above-the-knee skirt, the high heels.

"You wear that kind of stuff to work?"

Ignoring his question, she said, "We were just having some decaf. Come and join us." She turned on her heel and headed for the kitchen, not caring whether or not he'd follow. He did.

She retrieved another mug and poured him a serving. As she handed it to him, his mouth dropped open. He stared at her arm. No, her wrist.

The platinum bracelet.

"Where did you get that?" His voice sounded hoarse, as though he'd been rooting for the Phillies for both parts of a doubleheader.

Mustering all of her dignity, Lyssa set the mug on the table, at the place setting next to Kat, who to her credit, kept silent. "You left your bridal bed to ask me that?"

"Don't go trying to change the subject. *Where did you get that bracelet?*"

"Why are you shouting at me? And what difference does it make where I got this little trinket?" She delighted in copying the phrase that Peyton Savidge had used when he snapped it onto her wrist. "Bailey, Banks & Biddle maybe? Lord and Taylor? Tiffany's?" She deliberately picked up her own mug and took a slow sip, eyeing him over the rim. "Maybe it was a gift."

He grabbed her arm, splashing coffee onto the table. Kat shot to her feet and plucked the mug from Lyssa's hand before something more drastic happened. "That's the Platinum Society bracelet." George's voice dripped accusation.

Taken aback at this breach of secrecy, Lyssa stalled. "Platinum Society? What's that?"

"Don't be so coy. If you're wearing that thing, you know damn well what it is."

"Then why aren't you wearing one, since you seem to know what it is?"

"Hell, I've been trying for..." His voice trailed off as he apparently realized what he'd just admitted.

"And no one will sponsor you, isn't that right?" Lyssa tried not to smirk. Talk about poetic justice. "You're jealous!"

Undeterred, he attacked from a different direction. "You've been in a sex club behind my back?"

Lyssa couldn't help it. She burst out laughing. "Oh, George, you should see your face! That look is priceless!" She took a few steps back until her hip touched the counter, then leaned against it, grateful for its support while she indulged in more laughter. "Do you for one minute think that I'd have had enough gumption to bare myself—pardon the pun—to such naked scrutiny when you kept putting me down because I was so fat and sexless?"

He sputtered. "Then when did you—"

"George, we're divorced. I have the final decree to prove it. I don't have to answer to you for anything. Why should you care about my sex life? Don't you have one of your own? Of course, if the last ten years of our marriage was any indication, your bride probably is disappoin—"

His face purpled. "Shut up! Just shut up!"

"Hey, will you look at that." Obviously trying to defuse the situation, Kat jumped in, matching her wrist to Lyssa's and aligning the two gleaming platinum ribbons in front of the man.

George's eyes goggled. "Both of you?" he choked out. "Are you lesbians?"

Another bout of laughter weakened Lyssa's knees. Kat joined in, both of them laughing so hard, their mascara ran from the tears leaking from their eyes.

When she finally regained some semblance of composure, Lyssa pulled a tissue from the box on the counter and blotted under her eyes. "Well, if that threebie I told you about was two guys and a girl, you probably don't have to worry. But if it was one guy with me and another woman, or maybe three women, then you might well come to that conclusion."

Her eyes met Kat's. As if a signal passed between them, Kat moved forward and kissed Lyssa on the mouth, pressing her into the counter and rubbing her body up and down like a contented cat against Lyssa's body.

It didn't last long. Lyssa tried to get into the spirit of the thing, but laughter still bubbled out of her. Kat moved her face far enough away to meet Lyssa's eyes and she, too, began snickering at the joke they were playing on George. She turned to face him, resting her own butt against the counter, her arm encircling Lyssa's shoulder. "Wanna make another threebie, Georgie?" she cooed.

"You're mad, both of you," he managed, his eyes shifting from one smiling face to the other. "I can ruin your reputation with this thing."

All levity vanished. Lyssa's face hardened. "Don't you dare try. Why is it that you were able to walk all over me for so many years, and I try, once, to get your goat, and the first thing you do is want to strike back? Can't you stand not being the center of my life?"

"Damn you, I came here to offer a compromise!"

"About what?"

"Dartmouth tuition."

Every atom in Lyssa's body came to attention. Shrugging off Kat's hand, she pushed off from the counter and took a deliberate step forward. "What about it?" she asked through clenched teeth.

"You take out a second mortgage on your house to repay the tuition loan that Quick, Bowers & Savidge set up, and I'll make the payments."

"No. Uh-uh. No way. *You're* the one who's mad."

"Lyssie, think. There's so much equity in this house, you can get a mortgage from any bank in town. This is a good, solid house in a great location. You can—"

"How do you know," she overrode him in anger, "that I haven't already taken out a second or even a third mortgage? What do you think I'm living on in between commissions? Who do you think paid for all the things Michelle took with her to Dartmouth? All the clothes and the microwave and the desktop computer and printer and everything else on the list?"

George's face paled.

She wasn't finished. "And who are you to renege on a court order? To put your own daughter's future in jeopardy? When we agreed to the divorce, you pleaded with me to take the house so Michelle wouldn't be uprooted, but that's only because the stock market was still booming and you had a half million dollars in stocks and mutual funds that you didn't want to share. Don't you take it out on your own daughter if the market didn't keep going up and up into the stratosphere. If you weren't so greedy, you would have judiciously sold some stocks in time to meet your payment.

"And don't you threaten to smear my name." She took another step forward, forcing him to retreat a step. "Who do you think your lawyer will be? If you're going to say Quick, Bowers & Savidge, think again. They'll be on the side of the beneficiary whose future they hold in trust."

Lyssa took a deep breath. "Besides, you already owe the money to Quick, Bowers & Savidge, not to Dartmouth. I'm sure they have a better collection agency than I do. I wouldn't put it past you to stiff me out of a payment or three."

George opened his mouth to argue then snapped it shut.

"Get out of my house, George," she said in a deadly quiet voice. "I have complete faith in my daughter's attorneys. You will not swindle Michelle out of her college education."

"You'll regret this," he sputtered. Then turned on his heel and marched down the hall.

"Don't slam the door," she called as she followed to lock the door behind him.

Chapter Ten

Half asleep, Lyssa felt the sheet being tugged down, the warm cotton gliding sensuously over her nude body. The gentle abrasion caused her nipples to peak. Lower, and still lower it slid, caressing her hips, her thighs, every inch of her in soft, delicious friction. Her eyes fluttered open. The room was dark as sin.

"Who's there?" she whispered.

Silence.

The sheet tugged lower, until her calves, her ankles, her toes felt the slight wisp of a breeze. A strong hand clasped her left ankle, lifted her leg slightly. She felt her big toe encircled by a warm, moist mouth. She shivered.

"Savidge?"

"Don't think, just feel," a low, soft voice whispered.

Savidge. Lyssa felt her muscles relaxing. She hadn't realized how she'd tensed up at the sudden intrusion into her dreams. *Who else would it be?* she chided herself.

His slightly raspy tongue licked the inside of her arch. She sighed and concentrated on the delectable sensations. His tongue continued its leisurely exploration to the inside of her calf. When it reached her knee, he lifted her leg high enough to take tiny bites from the soft underside, exposing her crotch to the air, to his scrutiny. Lyssa felt her breath quicken at the thought. *No, it was too dark for him to see the most vulnerable part of her anatomy.*

She felt the bed dip under his weight as he slid between her knees, settling the raised leg on his shoulder. She could feel his hot breath raising goose bumps on her skin. His mouth tasted, nibbled, licked its way up her inner thigh. The dreamlike feeling escalated and liquid fire streaked to her crotch, her belly, her breasts. Her nipples ached to feel his mouth on them. Moisture gathered, seeped through her nether lips. Her hips lifted in silent invitation.

A purely masculine chuckle greeted that motion. The next thing she felt was a puff of air on her exposed crotch. Lyssa let out an involuntary cry. His answering groan was followed by his tongue licking the outer edges of her slit, up and down, teasing, torturing her. She grabbed a fistful of hair and tried to direct him to *there*, the spot that throbbed most with fire and wanting. She needed him to touch it, lick it, suck it until she exploded.

A harsh sound intruded in her ear. She tried to close her mind to it, to concentrate on her nocturnal visitor, but it rang stridently, interrupting the sensuous feelings that had been coursing through her.

The phone.

Damn. Lyssa opened her eyes to the darkness. It had been a dream. Savidge was in London. *Damn and double damn.*

As she groped for the bedside phone, she read the lighted numbers of the digital clock. One-ten. Her heart stuttered. No phone call in the middle of the night was ever good news.

She mumbled something that might have been "Hello."

"Are you naked?"

"Savidge?" Her heart thundered then resumed its normal beat. It wasn't bad news about Michelle.

"I am." It was a low rumble in her ear.

Was he acknowledging that he was Savidge? Or that he was naked? The thought sent a flutter through Lyssa.

"What are you wearing?"

"A smile," she murmured, deciding that he'd meant the latter.

"What are you doing?"

"You interrupted the most delicious dream." Her voice sounded sleepy, soft, sexy to her own ears. She stretched languorously, cradling the phone to her ear like a lover.

"Tell me about it."

"Wait a minute. Where are you?"

"London. It's just after six o'clock. I've been awake a while, thinking about you."

Lyssa processed this information. "So you waited until I fell asleep to call?"

He chuckled. "No, actually, I debated whether to call you at all." He paused then added, "But I had to hear your voice."

"Oh." She wasn't quite sure how to respond, so she didn't. But her toes curled.

"Tell me about your dream."

"Um, I was dreaming about you."

"Good. What were we doing?"

She could feel herself blush. Dare she tell him?

Of course she dared. Hadn't they already done things that would make a sailor blush?

"I was naked under the sheet and you pulled it down the length of my body. You were waking me up with your kisses all over me. I was just starting to enjoy all the sensations when you called."

"Good," he repeated. "Are you still naked?"

"Yes," she whispered, a little breathlessly.

"Will you do me a favor?" Was it her imagination, or did his voice sound hoarse?

"If I can."

"Touch your breast for me. I want to see your nipple get hard."

"I'm touching it. Rubbing my palm over the nipple."

"Tell me how it feels."

"Like electricity zapping down to my crotch. It tingles."

"Good. Now roll your nipple between your fingers. Pinch it. Pretend it's my mouth, my teeth. I'm tasting your tits and loving it."

"Savidge." Her breath came shorter as she followed his directive.

"Now run your fingers down your belly to your slit. I want you to pretend that's my tongue. Can you do that for me? Can you rub your finger up and down your clit?"

"*Savidge.*"

"Are you wet?"

"Yes." She could feel her chest heaving. She ached for his fingers, his mouth, right *there*, where she was drenched with moisture.

"I want you to—"

"Wait!" Thoughts of his hard, naked body next to her, inside her, slammed into her brain like the reverberation of thunder booming directly overhead. "I want you to tell me what *you're* doing."

His chuckle came through five thousand miles of night to tickle low in her belly. "I've got my hand on my cock, pretending it's you rubbing your hand up and down, slowly, from the base to the tip and back again, stroking, stroking. Your touch is like silk. It's making me even harder than I was a few minutes ago when I was thinking of you, wondering whether to call you."

Lyssa gulped. She could see the long, thick length of him in her hand, feel him in her mouth. Boldly she ordered, "Wet your finger and run it around the crown. Pretend it's my tongue. I want to feel it throb against my tongue."

A long moment went by before he said, "Lyssa. I want you."

She let her eyelids flutter closed. One hand was tweaking her nipple. The other dipped in and out of her slick passage. It was becoming difficult to hold the phone in place between her ear and her shoulder. "Savidge?"

"Hmmm?"

"Are you going to come?"

"Do you want me to?" Breathless, too.

"*Yes!*" She inserted a second finger into her vagina. "I want you to come with me. It's…I'm close…I want…"

"Lyssa." His voice sounded like a rusty nail. "I don't usually…masturbate…"

"Together," she whispered, her fingers moving more frantically now. "I want you inside me, fucking me. Picture yourself on top of me, your hips pumping harder and harder, faster and faster. Your cock sliding in and out. The friction is driving me crazy. My cunt is dripping wet, it's burning hot. I'm squeezing myself around your cock. It feels so good, having you inside me, ramming into me. It's building, I almost can't stand it, I'm ready to explode. Help me, Savidge. Help me go over the top."

"Oh God, Lyss." He took a long, shuddering breath. "I see your lush body. You're on top of me, those magnificent tits swinging near my face. I'm reaching up, catching one in my mouth. Sucking on it. Driving you wild. Driving *me* wild." A half-moan, half-laugh. "Feel my hands. I have a death grip on your hips, holding you so close you can't escape. I need you, need to fuck you, need to get deeper. I need to come in you. No condom, nothing between us. Just the feel of you around me."

His breathing became harsher. She could almost see the sweat at his hairline, the opaque look in his eyes that told her his climax was near.

"Need you." The last Lyssa could barely hear as his voice trailed into a long, guttural moan that sent her over the top with him. Stars exploded before her eyes, inside her head, her body. The phone slipped from her ear, but she could still hear him gasping, breathing hard like a wild creature after a chase.

And she was the prey.

Or maybe he was. It was difficult to think right now.

Chapter Eleven

"Evann said you wanted to see me as soon as I got here. What's up?"

"Come in, Lyssa. Close the door."

Wary at his autocratic tone, Lyssa shut the door behind her and gazed at her office manager seated at his sleekly modern desk. Orson Ames had been most generous with his guidance over the year she'd been employed there, had taught her how to handle the most finicky client, how to subtly call attention to any noteworthy features in a particular dwelling so that the client felt it was a must-have feature.

Now his mien was stern, almost judicial. The gray of his eyes under horn-rimmed glasses looked like unbending steel. The frown lines over his eyebrows made deep creases in his weathered skin.

"Prestige Realty has received a very serious complaint against you, Lyssa. We have to resolve this before I can allow you to interact with any of our clients."

Lyssa took an involuntary breath. Having the potted schefflera in the corner burst into flame wouldn't have surprised her more.

"I don't understand. Did I offend someone? How? Who was it?" She rummaged through her brain for a list of the people she'd shown homes to over the past few months. None of her clients had given her the slightest inkling that she'd said or done anything in the least provocative or unprofessional.

"Please sit down." Orson raked his left hand through thinning brownish hair. His wedding ring gleamed briefly in the afternoon sunlight leaking through half-drawn blinds.

Without taking her gaze off his, Lyssa groped for the armrest of one of the captain's chairs in front of his desk and sat down warily. "What did I do?"

"Mind you, I don't believe it, but still, I had to tell Halsey."

Dread settled in the pit of Lyssa's stomach. Halsey Smythe was the president of Prestige Realty, owner of a dozen real estate offices scattered throughout the prestigious Philadelphia suburbs of Chester and Montgomery counties. She'd only met him once, at the company's Christmas party. He was a big, dour-faced individual who looked as if he had a peptic ulcer.

"Tell him what? For God's sake, Orson, spit it out! What am I accused of?"

He sighed heavily. "Moral turpitude."

It took a moment for Lyssa's brain synapses to respond. "Moral turpitude?"

George! Was this his way of getting back at her for wearing the platinum bracelet? If so, he hadn't wasted any time. She'd arrived at one because today was her turn to work the evening shift. She'd spent the morning mooning over Savidge as she did hand laundry. Her fingers gripped the armrests of the chair until her knuckles turned white. She wished it was George's scrawny neck under her fists.

"Who was it, my ex-husband?" she spat out.

Orson's face registered surprise. "George Markham? Good grief, no. Where did you get that idea?"

Stricken, Lyssa sputtered, "I just thought—"

Her next thought was worse. "Then who?"

Orson shuffled papers on his desk. "Ah, here it is. Evann took the call first thing this morning, said the woman insisted on talking to the president of the company, but she eventually settled for the highest-ranking person in this office. Made me promise to tell Halsey or she'd go to the newspapers with it. Woman by the name of—" he adjusted his glasses on his fleshy nose and peered at the lined yellow sheet he'd used to make notes. "Sally Greene."

The blood drained from Lyssa's face. She could feel herself becoming lightheaded. "You've got to be kidding. I don't even know anyone named Sally Greene. Moral turpitude? What's she talking about? Who is she? Give me her address, her phone number. I'll go right down there and set her straight."

"Now, Lyss, it's gone beyond that. This is a serious accusation. Have you ever heard of the Platinum Society?"

Lyssa fought to keep her composure. It *had* to be George. Who else knew about the club?

She scrutinized Orson's face. Not a twitch in his stern mouth, not a hint of smile in his unblinking eyes. His face had always been open, honest. She'd thought more than once that he would never make a good poker player. So he couldn't possibly know about the club.

Should she lie? How much should she admit?

"What—what kind of club is it?" She decided to fudge.

"According to this lady, they host orgies every night. Naked men and women doing who knows what. Whips, chains, handcuffs." Various shades of pink crept into his cheeks as he spoke. "Indiscriminate coupling in threes and fours, she said, and daisy chains—whatever that is—and other, well, here's her words verbatim, 'unthinkable, despicable acts'." His face was now totally red.

Lyssa was feeling pretty uncomfortable herself. How could she speak of this to someone who obviously had never participated?

"And that's not the worst of it," he continued. "She claims you were seen leaving one of these, as she called it, 'establishments' at about three o'clock in the morning."

"No way," Lyssa said. "The only time in the past year—that is, since my divorce—that I've been to anything that might be considered an 'establishment' was this week, when a friend—" her voiced wobbled on the word "—and I went to a jazz club in downtown Philly. I will, however, admit that it was about one-thirty when we left. This *establishment*—" she emphasized the word "—is public."

Unvoiced was the realization that she had no clue what time it had been when she'd left Peyton Savidge's orgy. But it was a home, not an "establishment". And she'd worn her mask all night, so there was no way she could have been fingered, especially since she'd slunk down low in the BMW as Kat drove them home.

"I'm sorry." Orson peeled his glasses off his face and set them on top of the yellow sheet. "She said that someone like that, ushering unsuspecting men and women into strangers' bedrooms, well, she shuddered to think what kinds of unspeakable suggestions could be made by someone with whom these people had an unwritten pact to be aboveboard and honest, not to—"

"But I've never—"

"I know. You wouldn't—couldn't—be like that. You're too genteel, too sweet. I don't think I've ever heard a swear word from your mouth. And you don't wear short skirts or tight sweaters. You don't walk with a wiggle. You're friendly but not overbearing or suggestive in any way. You've never shown the slightest bit of sexuality in this office."

Lyssa bit the inside of her mouth to keep from responding. Is that how the world had seen her for the nineteen years she'd been married to George? A sexless, colorless lump who blended in with the woodwork?

But she *had* been a sexless, colorless lump. Still, the accusation of moral turpitude hurt. She *liked* her newly discovered sensuality, the freedom to express herself. "I'd like to talk to her, to ask her how she came about this information."

"Depends on what Halsey says."

"But surely I can talk to her, get this straightened out before we have to involve him." The sour expression he'd worn at the Christmas party burned itself into her brain. Halsey Smythe would no doubt align himself with her accuser.

"Too late." Orson lifted his arm, checked his leather-banded watch. "He should be here any minute."

Lyssa swallowed. "Halsey Smythe is coming here?" She was toast. He'd never visited this office while Lyssa had been present. As far as she knew, he oversaw his managerial staff with weekly meetings at the corporate office. Oh God, how could she keep Michelle from discovering why she'd been fired?

A polite knock at the door interrupted her dire thoughts.

"Come in," Orson said, and stood in anticipation of greeting his guest.

Taking her cue, Lyssa also stood, awaiting her sentence like a convicted criminal before a hanging judge.

When Halsey Smythe strode into the office, the space around her seemed to diminish. A tall, thick-set bear of a man with a gleaming bald pate and bushy dark eyebrows and mustache to match, Smythe nodded a hello to Orson, then turned his brown-eyed gaze to her.

Lyssa steeled herself not to tremble in his presence. This man held her future in his hands. Did she need a lawyer? Would she perjure herself to save her job?

He stretched out a hand. "Lyssa. I remember our discussion at the Christmas party. You have a daughter, had her heart set on some school up in New England, right?"

Heartened that he had remembered something personal about her, Lyssa relaxed fractionally and accepted the handshake. Her hand felt swallowed up in his huge paw.

"Yes. She started at Dartmouth this very week."

"Good for her. Congratulations." He gestured Lyssa to sit, then took the other chair. It was just barely big enough for his girth.

"Well, let's not beat around the bush. I'm sure Orson's told you of this woman's allegations. Hell, I can see it in your face. Listen, don't let it get to you. Some people have nothing better to do than to make trouble. Orson, what do you think we should do?"

Orson cleared his throat. "She did threaten to go public. I'm sure Lyssa isn't guilty of these unbelievable allegations. Maybe we can talk the Board of Realtors out of a license suspension, but if the woman persists in making trouble, she could talk to the daily rag and splatter mud all over Prestige Realty's name. That's your call."

"But if she *was* guilty…?"

Lyssa bristled. Would she be tarred and feathered without having a say? The words burned the inside of her mouth, but she remained silent.

Orson steepled his fingers and pressed them against his pursed mouth, elbows on the padded armrests of his chair. He stared at a spot on the carpeted floor between the two captain's chairs for a moment. "She's a good agent. She just brought in a three-million-dollar listing. I've gotten great feedback from that persnickety Mrs. Peifer about what a nice person she is. I'm sure we could get a lot of character references for her if we had to go to the Board of Realtors to plead her case."

He looked at Smythe. "Maybe Prestige Realty would like to spend a few bucks on a private investigator, see who this Sally Greene character is. What makes her tick. Meanwhile, Lyssa'd have to keep a low profile for a few days, a week maybe, in case this woman is obsessed with making trouble."

Dismayed, Lyssa held her tongue. A week without seeing clients meant a week without a possible commission. But it was more than she could have hoped for a few minutes ago. It sounded as though she could keep her job.

Halsey Smythe broke into a smile. "Capital idea. We have someone on retainer. I'll get him right on it."

He turned his overly large body to face Lyssa, no mean feat within the confines of the captain's chair, and raised his right hand to stroke his long, thick mustache. His eyes bored into hers. "I think we can settle this without too much trouble."

Lyssa stared at that right hand. His wrist, to be exact.

She saw what had been hidden underneath his finely tailored French cuff. A thin platinum bracelet identical to the one she'd hidden in her jewelry case.

* * * * *

"Did I wake you?"

The sexy timbre of Savidge's voice slid down Lyssa's spine like a hot tongue. She had snuggled into cool flowered sheets a few minutes ago, after the ten o'clock news. "Mmmm. I was just falling asleep."

"How was your day?"

"Good and bad. The good was, the video of your home is in the can. Took a couple of hours. The tech was very professional, knew just what I wanted. We should have a rough cut in a few days." Lyssa settled herself deeper between the silky sheets. "By the way, I found something when I was fluffing up a pillow."

"Oh? Which pillow?"

"One of those blood-red damask ones on the eggshell sofa in the living room."

Savidge chuckled low in his throat. "Couldn't have been a used condom. We haven't made love in my house yet."

Sparks singed every nerve ending in Lyssa's body. She could vividly imagine the weight of him pressing her into the nubby texture of the sofa cushions. Darn, but he could make her yearn for him in the blink of an eye.

"Actually, it was a piece of jewelry." She held her breath to see what he'd say.

"Hmm. I don't remember anything being missing."

"It was a bracelet."

A few beats went by before he repeated, "A bracelet?"

"Yes. A thin platinum one with intricate engravings."

"What kind of engravings?"

Was he playing coy? Did he not want her to know about the "secret signal"? "I didn't have a jeweler's loupe with me, so I couldn't make it out. They were intricate, sinuous lines, that's all I could see."

She had, however, scrutinized her own bracelet under a magnifying glass when she'd returned home. The carvings depicted various coupling positions that had probably been lifted from the Kama Sutra. Her cheeks heated to think what Orson Ames might say if he saw one on her wrist.

"Finders, keepers," he said. She imagined him shrugging.

"Actually, I have one of my own."

She heard him take a deep breath. "You do?"

"Yes. I'll show it to you when you get back."

"Like the one you found?"

"Yes." She decided to take the plunge. "Your father gave it to me after the board voted me in. He's a great kisser, by the way."

This time his pause was longer. "If you're trying to make me jealous, you're succeeding."

The sentiment warmed Lyssa down to her toes, but she couldn't let him know how pleased she was. "Peyton? He seems to be a nice man. I can see where his son got some of his more, shall we say, appealing traits."

"'Nice'. I think he'd raise an eyebrow at that description."

"I only saw him for a few minutes."

"Probably because you were blindfolded the rest of the time."

Lyssa smiled, remembering. "I was very apprehensive. Kat didn't tell me what to expect. She just peremptorily told me 'you're wearing it and shut up and come with me'."

He chuckled. "I can imagine Kat doing just that."

"The screening committee all seemed very caring."

"They are. They're people with hopes and dreams and fears, just like you and me." A pause. "Peyton is available, you know. The most eligible bachelor in the Fortune Five Hundred."

"Not interested. He does, however, have something that I like."

A beat went by before he asked, "What's that?"

How much should she admit? They couldn't see each other, but had already shared so much. In the cocoon of darkness and flowered sheets, the intimacy was almost unbearably sweet. "His son."

"Good." She heard him swallow. "Lyss, I'm not sure I'm happy that you've been accepted into the Platinum Society."

"Oh? Why not?"

His voice turned hoarse. "I saw you rubbing the bacon with the fireman, the cowboy. Now that I know you—not Salome, but *you*, Lyssa Markham—I'm not sure I could watch you go from man to man and not want to wring his neck."

"Savidge," she whispered the name like a prayer.

He cleared his throat then said briskly, "Enough of that. You said your day was good and bad. What's the bad?"

It took her a moment to switch gears. Had she imagined the emotion in his voice? The jealousy he was trying to minimize? Was he hiding embarrassment that he'd said too much? Okaaaay, she'd do the same.

"Sally Greene. Some woman who complained that I was guilty of moral turpitude."

"You're kidding. Who in today's world uses words like that?"

"She must have looked it up in a law book. I thought it was George. He saw Kat's and my bracelets, and we kind of made fun of him." She related the incident in her kitchen where she and Kat had briefly explored lesbianism in front of George's goggling eyes.

"He could still be behind it," Savidge mused. "The man strikes me as being a dog in a manger. Doesn't want it, but doesn't want anyone else to have it, either."

"That's for sure. I pity his poor bride."

"So you're not jealous that he remarried?"

"Jealous? Of him? Of them? Good grief, no! Shedding him was the best thing I've ever done! Correction. Second best. The best was letting Kat talk me into going to a very special masquerade."

"I bless her every day for that selfless act."

"Me, too. It's opened my eyes to what I can be. What I *am*. I love my sensuality, my freedom of expression. I want to taste and touch everything. I want to expose myself to everything the world has to offer."

Savidge was silent a long time. Lyssa wondered if the connection to London had faded. Or if he'd construed her words to mean she wanted to expose herself to every *man* in the world and he didn't like the idea. Finally he said, "You deserve all of those things. Tell me, what was the upshot of this accusation of moral turpitude?"

A twinge of disappointment darted through her, then she chided herself. They had made no vows of fidelity to each other. She mimicked his casual air. "It was the strangest thing. Halsey Smythe, the president and owner of Prestige Realty, he came to the office to talk to me and Orson, my manager. Orson, poor guy, had to tell me all of what she said. His cheeks, his ears, they turned red as a fire engine. It was obvious he wasn't a member.

"Anyway, this woman threatened to go to the press with the story of me being seen in an 'establishment'—her word—that catered to the depraved and the promiscuous. Orson, bless his heart, didn't know anything about the Platinum Society, but he still stood up for me. Halsey agreed to pay for a private investigator to snoop around Sally Greene, then he lifted his hand up to stroke his mustache. Savidge, he was wearing the same bracelet!

"I can't tell you how relieved I was. He was so subtle about it, too. Orson didn't suspect a thing. If I hadn't accepted the offer to join, I wouldn't have known about the bracelets, wouldn't know it was the 'secret signal' among members. And I'd have still been tarred and feathered and not known I had an ally."

"I'm glad for you," he said, his tone subdued. "You'll have lots of friends in the Platinum Society."

He almost sounded regretful, Lyssa thought. As if he really didn't want her to be a member. *Could* he be jealous of other men? Of the thought she might want to spend a night or a week with another man or two?

It was time to get onto less weighty ground.

"How much longer will you be in London?"

"I should complete my business today, then I'm going to Cambridge to see my son. I'll be back on Saturday."

"Will you have jet lag?"

"London's only five hours' difference. Why? Want to invite me to dinner?"

I want to invite you into my bed! She gave a little, self-conscious laugh. "If you don't mind second-rate cooking. I'm not sure I could measure up to Yuki's expertise."

"Omelets would be fine."

Lyssa's heart skipped. He wanted to see her! She didn't have to pretend to be a fancy chef, but she'd certainly give him something tasty. Even if she had to con Kat into giving her a pair of her candy-pants for Savidge to lick.

After a few more minutes of desultory conversation, Savidge said goodnight without a hint of phone sex.

She wondered why she was so disappointed.

Chapter Twelve

"Damn you, George, what the heck do you think you're doing?"

"Whoa. You can't come storming into my office like that!"

Lyssa waved the objection aside. "Your assistant's been here for eight years. She does recognize me, you know. She was on the phone and just motioned me to go in."

George ran a finger around the collar of his beige, button-down-collared shirt. Good. She hoped his noose would feel even tighter when she got done.

"Sit down. You make me nervous." George flopped into his high-backed executive chair and put his hands, palms down, on his blotter, as if needing to feel something solid between himself and a formidable adversary. Which she was, now that she had found some backbone.

"I'll say just two words to you." Spine straight, Lyssa sat in the guest chair across from him. "Sally Greene."

George's eyelid twitched. "Who's that?"

"Don't you 'who's that' me. You know damn well that Sally Greene is your new mother-in-law." She'd have bet her next commission that there was a link to her sneaky ex. It hadn't taken long for Halsey's PI to discover the connection.

"Oh," he said, apparently stalling for time. "*That* Sally Greene."

"You put her up to it, didn't you." It wasn't a question. She was damned sure he had. "How come I never saw how petty you were? You don't get your way, you take your baseball and go home."

"Now, Lyssie, don't get your knickers in a knot. I might have mentioned it to my wife that you belonged to a sex club, and she might have told her mother. Sally didn't tell me until afterwards what she'd done."

"My name is Lyssa. Don't you ever call me Lyssie again. And how would Sally Greene know what to say unless someone told her what the Platinum Society was? Or maybe she's a member, and embellished on what you told her because she'd experienced it firsthand. Is that it? Should I tell your bride what her mother knew about the Platinum Society? The daisy chain and all the other variations of fucking I was told she mentioned?"

To his credit, George kept his voice moderate, even though he winced that a certain four-letter word appeared in the same breath as his mother-in-law's name. "Couldn't you have just called me? This isn't quite worth you coming all the way downtown just to ask me some questions. And you've acquired a dirty mouth."

Lyssa leaned forward in her chair. "No dirtier than your mother-in-law's. I wanted to see your lying eyes when you denied knowing any of this crap. I learned to read your eyes a long time ago. Remember you told me that when you were a kid, you were afraid to look into your mother's eyes when you'd done something wrong? She always said she could see crosses in your eyes when you lied. You know something? She was right. Because I could, too."

"Babe, listen—"

"Don't you 'Babe' me." She stood, planted her fists on her side of his desk and loomed over him. "I'm no longer the doormat you turned me into. I've got a spine now. In fact, I've got more balls than you have. And I'll use them if I need to." She had the satisfaction of seeing him flinch.

"Before you try to stab me in the back again, think carefully on this." She poked a finger into his hand still splayed on the blotter, resisting the urge to crash a fist down onto his fingers. "If you're not a member, you don't know who else is. I do. I can access the roster in a minute. You'd be surprised who'll be on my side in any altercation you care to start."

She took a breath, relishing the gaping mouth, the bugged-out eyes of her ex.

"For example. Do you know if any members of your investment firm are Platinum Society members? What would you say if some night, when I'm doing the nasty with one or two of your naked partners, I let it slip that George Markham is embezzling? Or that you're a faggot who likes to be whipped by a bald giant?"

She had the satisfaction of watching his Adam's apple bobble a few times as his face paled to almost the shade of his teeth.

"You wouldn't," he managed.

A nasty smile in danger of turning into a sneer crept onto Lyssa's face. "Don't bet on it."

With that, she spun on her heel and strode to the door. When she opened it, she turned back to him, knowing her grin had turned to pure evil.

"Or maybe your little MariBeth is a member."

And had the pleasure of slamming the door against the sight of his now-purple face.

* * * * *

The satisfaction of one-upping George faded as Lyssa scrutinized the platinum bracelet she'd found under the blood-red damask pillow in Savidge's living room. She didn't know what had possessed her to inspect it under a magnifying glass. Sitting in her bedroom, thinking of him, perhaps she just needed something of his to touch, to hold near to her heart, her lips. And it comforted her to know that he didn't have his "secret handshake" for entrée into the London club.

A stone lodged in her throat when she read the engraving inside of the bracelet. CYS. Quickly she opened her jewelry case and retrieved her own bracelet. Sure enough, LMM was inscribed inside. The powers that be in the Club had done their research. She didn't use a middle initial in professional or legal matters, so they had used her maiden name, McBride.

Savidge's ex-wife was named Columba, Kat had told her, one of the well-heeled Younts of Bryn Mawr. But didn't Kat also tell her they'd divorced six years ago? If so, had the bracelet lain hidden under the pillows for that long?

She scoffed at the idea. Surely he'd had a maid or cleaning service over the years for a home that large. Someone would have found it in all that time.

Or had he indulged in a quickie with Columba recently? Was that why the first thing he'd said when she told him what she'd found was, "It wasn't a used condom"? Because he hadn't needed one? Because maybe she'd had a hysterectomy and he knew she could no longer conceive?

And why was she worrying? Just because she couldn't stomach the idea of having sex with her ex-husband, anyone would be crazy not to want to indulge in the same with Savidge. Especially an ex-wife, who presumably knew of his expertise firsthand.

Damn. Savidge had really gotten under her skin. Not just the sex, mind-blowing though it was. The man intrigued her. Coming to her rescue at the pool when George confronted her, and when he'd reneged on paying the tuition. Dinner at Savidge's home, his thoughtfulness in having Kat bring the overnight case for her to use. Dancing close in that smoky jazz joint. His tender smile when he'd awakened her in the Aston Martin at two in the morning. Kissing her until her knees buckled and then leaving her wanting more. Calling her from London just to hear her voice.

Images crowded her mind of Savidge fucking her on his desk at the law office, then later on the bathroom counter, of his tongue on her slit when she lay naked and sheened with sweat after her dance of the seven veils. Even the phone sex had been special, something she'd never even considered until after she'd met him.

She let her eyelids flutter closed. *Savidge.* She was hooked. She didn't know if she'd ever be able to attend another club function if she thought Savidge would turn his attention to someone else. It would break her heart to watch him in action if she was just one of the crowd, or worse yet, merely a former lover.

He had admitted over the phone that he was jealous, but that reference was to his father's kissing her, wasn't it? Then he'd briskly changed the subject, as though getting into an emotional quagmire was something to be avoided on pain of death.

Well, she'd play it out the same cool way. The phrase "fuck each other's brains out" now made sense to her. She'd do it whatever way, whenever, however he wanted it, because, she admitted to herself, she was addicted to it. To him. And when the time came for him to walk out of her life, she'd deal with it then. Not a moment before.

But she'd be damned if she'd ask him how that bracelet came to be under the pillow.

Chapter Thirteen

"I brought you something."

Lyssa feasted her eyes on the man standing on her front porch, jacket slung over one shoulder, overnighter at his feet. He'd been gone less than a week, but it felt like a year since she'd seen him. Bruised smudges under his eyes, hair rumpled as though he'd run his fingers through it in agitation, the lines bracketing his mouth a little deeper. The creases in his black pin-striped trousers had disappeared. The three top buttons on his light blue shirt were unbuttoned, exposing a thatch of chest hair that made her fingers itch to grab a handful.

"Come in." Her voice felt thick. She stepped aside and allowed him to enter first, then closed and locked the door.

He spun her around, enveloped her in a bear hug. "God, I've missed you." His mouth descended to hers, and he kissed her like a dehydrated man in a desert who had found a waterhole, sucking and nibbling, thrusting his tongue in and out, ravaging her mouth.

When he released her mouth to kiss her throat, she murmured his name. She ran her hands up and down his back, following the contours of his narrow hips to his taut butt, pulling him closer to her.

After a few minutes of foreplay that made them almost spontaneously combust, he slid his hands to her upper arms and pulled her back just enough to gaze into her eyes, his Harrison Ford smile aimed at her. "Miss me?"

Lyssa took a deep, stabilizing breath. "About as much as you missed me."

"Good thing you closed the door. We wouldn't want any of your neighbors to have heart attacks."

"Would you like some coffee?"

"Sounds great. I'm sorry I couldn't make dinner," he said as they turned to walk down the hall to the kitchen, his arm slung casually across her shoulder, hers around his waist. "I came right from the airport. Had to take a commercial flight, and it had engine trouble. I spent three hours on the ground at Heathrow, wishing I hadn't been so magnanimous as to allow my partner to use the Lear jet."

"You own your own jet?" she asked as she spooned hazelnut Colombian into the Braun.

"The firm does. I don't use it often. I'm admitted to practice in Pennsylvania, New York, Illinois and California. I usually fly commercial in the U.S."

"What were you doing in London?" Lyssa could have bitten her tongue as soon as the question came out of her mouth. It was none of her business, she chastised herself as she plugged the pot into the electrical outlet. And she would *not* ask him if he visited the London Platinum Society.

"We're working on a big merger. Our client gave me carte blanche to negotiate, and I was able to forge an agreement acceptable to all parties." His pleased smile erased the tiredness she'd seen in his eyes, but not the dark smudges under them.

"Congratulations," she said. "It must give you a great deal of satisfaction to complete a big deal."

"Not nearly as much as a certain woman who in my fantasies is wearing nothing but Shalimar and a smile."

Lyssa's breath hitched. He remembered her perfume.

She twirled a pirouette in front of him. "And here you're stuck with a barefoot woman who's wearing jeans and a T-shirt."

"Snug jeans and snugger T-shirt. Looks good to me, woman."

The burbling of the pot signaled that the coffee was ready. Lyssa busied herself pouring two cups, not wanting him to see how pleased she was at his comment. Because he hadn't wanted any phone sex during the second call, she'd vowed that he would have to make the next move.

When she had stirred cream into hers—he took his black—she served them both and sat beside him at the kitchen table. "You must be exhausted."

"Not too tired to be with you. Anything happening on the moral turpitude front?"

"You'll never guess who Sally Greene is."

Savidge set down his coffee cup. "Judging by the twinkle in your eyes, it's a killer answer."

"You got that right. She's George's new mother-in-law!"

He chuckled. "I might have guessed. So did this Smythe fellow call Mrs. Greene?"

"He didn't have to." Lyssa's mouth compressed into a determined line. "I confronted George in his office. Told him if he bothered me any more, I'd tell one of his investment buddies whose name I saw on the membership roster that he's a faggot who likes to be whipped by a bald giant."

Savidge threw back his head and roared with laughter. She joined in. It felt good to laugh with him, to share things with him. Like an old married couple who were still interested in what the other had experienced.

When the laughter petered out, she asked, "How did you get involved in the Platinum Society?"

Savidge raised his eyes to the ceiling, as if trying to decide where to start. "I had known Dad was involved with it in some fashion, but I didn't get pulled into it until after my divorce. Columba wasn't a bad woman, we just grew in different directions. We stuck together until our son graduated high school. We were living separate lives by then, so splitting was just the next step."

He drained his cup and set it on the table. "I was at loose ends. I was tired of all the arm candy wanting to be the next Mrs. Robert Savidge. I didn't know what I was looking for, but it certainly wasn't another marriage. Dad invited me to a party at his place, gave me some hint as to what it was.

"He'd always been a good father, even though I didn't see him for days or weeks at a time. But when he was home, he made it a point to teach me to sail, to read the stock quotes, talk about the birds and bees. I remember I was about ten years old when he winked at me, and said, 'You don't stop fucking just because you hit forty. Your mom and I still...' And then he stopped, as if embarrassed to be telling his prepubescent son something he probably wasn't ready to hear.

"But I never forgot that.

"So I went, not quite sure what to expect. Mom had died a few years before that. Coronary embolism. Went in a flash."

"Oh, Savidge, I'm sorry." Instinctively Lyssa reached out to touch his hand.

He shrugged. "It's how she would have wanted to go. No pain, no dragging on. She'd watched her own mother die by inches with cancer. Mom stayed around just long enough to tell us once more that she loved us."

Quietly Lyssa rose and filled his cup. He nodded absently in acknowledgement.

"Anyway, when I got to this party, it was a turn-on, of course. It's like living your wildest fantasy. But I couldn't just jump in. When all was said and done, to me it was akin to cruising the red-light district for a hooker."

He took her hand, entwined their fingers. "I'm not going to say I was a monk. Once I got to know the players, I did participate on occasion. Problem was the women started calling me, wanting to take it to the next level. So I started helping Dad police the affairs. I guess Kat explained. Someone's always the 'designated driver' who doesn't participate. He or she wanders around watching to see if anyone's eyes are panicky."

A smile played around the edges of his mouth. "When Dad got released from his responsibility, it was heartening to see that he still had the verve to go after one or another of the younger women. Younger for him, that is. He never wanted to look pathetic, chasing after a twenty-year-old like some of those former leading men in Hollywood who should be playing grandfathers. I've seen him on occasion with a well-turned-out widow of, oh, I'd guess in her late forties. A fifteen-year difference doesn't raise so many eyebrows."

Comfortable silence descended as they sat next to each other at the table, fingers still entwined. *I could get used to this*, Lyssa thought.

She brought Savidge's hand to her mouth and kissed the palm, then set it against her cheek. "You look tired. I guess you've had a long day."

"Long week." He stroked her mouth with his thumb. "It's good to be back."

"London was that bad?"

The sparkle in his eyes did funny things to her heart. "London was fine. This—" he grabbed her hand and tugged firmly until she had to rise off her chair, "—is better."

Somehow she found herself perched on his lap sideways, with his arms loosely clasped around her waist. His gaze, tenderly amused just a moment ago, turned intense. "Lyssa. I want to kiss you."

Her mouth quirked upward. "Don't let me stop you."

Bringing one hand up to cup her head, he nudged her until their lips were almost, but not quite, touching. "There's only one problem."

Her gaze lingering on his sexy mouth, she ventured, "You're too tired?"

"No way. You give me strength. You make me *want* to stay awake."

"Then...?"

"I can't stop with just one kiss."

As if to prove his point, he closed the gap between them, gently flicking his tongue across her mouth. Reflexively she opened it, softening, melding to him, twisting her shoulders to press her breasts against his chest, squirming on his lap to seat herself better atop his burgeoning cock. She tasted the coffee on his tongue, inhaled faint traces of woodsy aftershave and rumpled traveler.

More. She wanted more. More kisses, more body contact. Too many clothes, her mind said, while her body enjoyed the pure heaven of his lips as he intensified the kiss, angling his head to delve deeper into her mouth. Her arms went around his neck. She wished she could stand up to straddle him, to spread her legs wide to feel the hard bulge of him rubbing against her slit, but it felt too good just the way they were, his hands on her hips, pressing, rocking them.

His mouth nibbled hot, biting kisses down her throat and lower, until he latched onto one T-shirt-covered breast. She gave a soft moan, arching her back to offer him better access, and was rewarded when his hands crept under the soft, well-washed cotton.

"Lord save me," he groaned when his fingers reached the naked curve of her breast. "There oughta be a law against going braless when a man's trying to do the right thing."

"You're doing exactly the right thing." She grabbed the hem of her shirt and lifted it, abrading her already swollen nipple to a harder peak and exposing both breasts to his greedy gaze.

"So beautiful," he murmured, capturing first one, then the other nipple in his hot mouth and suckling like a starving infant.

Lyssa gloried in the sensations streaking through all her nerve endings as he tugged and licked, squeezed and then scraped his teeth lightly over each nipple. She placed her palms at his temples to hold him even closer as she whispered his name over and over.

"I can't stand this," he rasped, standing suddenly and setting her on her feet. Quickly he unsnapped the brass button, pulled down the zipper of her jeans, and knelt before her as he slipped the denim down her legs. "I need to taste you." He slid his fingers under the elastic of her panties and yanked the crotch aside.

Lyssa was just sane enough to think, *Why wasn't I wearing my sexy underwear?* when Savidge licked the cunt lips he'd just exposed, and all other thought fled. Her knees buckled and he lifted her by the waist to set her on top of the kitchen table.

He wrenched her jeans off one foot, leaving the garment dangling at her other ankle. He spread her knees and, grabbing the panty crotch again, brought the full impact of his mouth to bear on her slit. She leaned back on her elbows and opened her legs wide, barely hearing the sharp sound of breaking china as a cup crashed to the floor.

"Oh, God, Savidge, I've missed you, missed *this*." Lyssa lifted her legs onto his shoulders to allow him fuller access as he sucked her nub, tongued her slit, kneaded her ass cheeks.

Her climax took her unawares. She'd wanted the delicious feel of his mouth on her cunt to last a long time, but her fevered body demanded otherwise. She clamped her knees together, trapping his head, his mouth, as she bucked against him, gasping, raising her hips rhythmically as violent spasms exploded inside her.

When her breathing slowed down and her heartbeat neared normal, she slid her legs off his shoulders and sighed. "Welcome home, Savidge."

"Home." He smiled that lopsided smile and planted a quick kiss on the triangle of blonde hair on her pubis, then released the elastic. "Has a nice sound to it."

Savidge bent down to gather her other pant-leg, held it out for her to slip her foot into the opening. "Here. Get yourself dressed. Don't you want to see what I brought you from Harrod's?"

Frowning, Lyssa shimmied into her jeans. "Don't I get a chance?"

"You mean you want another pop even before you see your present?"

"No, dammit." She made a moue. "Didn't it occur to you that I might want to do unto you as you have done unto me?"

Tenderly, Savidge placed his palms on her cheeks, then kissed her forehead. "This isn't about me. I wanted to do this for you, not for me. I can live with a hard-on."

"Wait a minute." Lyssa poked his chest with her index finger. "What's sauce for the goose blah, blah, blah. You wanted to make me come. Okay, you did and I liked it. But you're saying you're too selfish to let me return the favor? You'd rather go home with blue balls than have a good fuck?"

"That's not it at all. I simply — "

"You know what I think? I think you got too much pussy in that London club. Between that and your jet lag, you can't perform and you don't want me to see you in that unflattering light. You want me to keep thinking of you as a hot stud in high demand."

"Honey, listen." Savidge gathered her into his arms. "I just—"

"Don't you 'honey' me." Lyssa tried to push herself away, but met with the immovable object of his chest.

"You look so cute when you're angry."

"That's patronizing."

A sheepish look crept over his face. "You're right. It was." Then a smile replaced it. "Hey, we're having our first lovers' quarrel."

Lyssa couldn't help it. She started to laugh. "You're incorrigible."

"I'm serious, Lyss. I want to be with you, I want us to do things that normal couples do. It doesn't always have to be sex. I want to wake up with you, go to sleep with you—and I mean make some 'z's', not a euphemism for sex. Although I want that, too. Lots of it. I want to bring you breakfast in bed and hot cocoa at night. I want to take you to the zoo and to the opera. I want to teach you to sail."

"Oh, Savidge…" Lyssa's voice dwindled to nothing. The lump in her throat prevented further speech. It sounded almost as if…

No, she dared not allow herself to think that they had a future together. He was too good to be true. Someone like Robert Savidge, rich, handsome, with a commanding presence and formidable intellect, what would he want with her?

His lips lightly brushed hers. "Lyssa, will you—"

The sound of metal clinking jolted her. "Who—what—"

Instantly Savidge pushed her protectively behind him. "Stay here. I'll go see. Sounds like someone's trying to get in."

The front door banged open. "Mom? It's me, Michelle. I need my laptop."

Lyssa's hand flew to her mouth. *Oh God, what if she'd come home ten minutes earlier?* She could feel her cheeks burn at the thought of her daughter seeing what they'd done on the kitchen table.

The cup! Hadn't she heard, in some dim corner of her mind, the sound of a cup breaking while they were engaging in an act that her daughter had better not have any knowledge of? Quickly she checked the state of her hair by running her fingers through her tresses. *Not too bad.* She could hear Michelle's voice getting louder as she strode down the hall toward the kitchen.

"I appreciate you letting me take your new one, Mom, but it doesn't dock to the PC that I have in my room the way my old one does, and I need to transfer all my notes from — "

Michelle stopped dead in her tracks, her mouth making a wide oval as she assimilated the fact that a tall, handsome stranger stood leaning casually against her mother's kitchen counter, one hand in his pants pocket in a partially successful attempt to hide the telltale bulge at his zipper, his attire rumpled and in dire need of pressing.

Speechless, she turned to her mother, both accusation and question in her eyes. Lyssa forced herself not to squirm under the microscopic inspection as she took mental tally of herself — T-shirt modestly pulled down to hips, jeans buttoned and zipped, hair tucked behind ears, barefoot —

"Hey, whose overnight bag is that?"

Lyssa stiffened as George came charging into the kitchen like an irritated rhino. He zeroed in on Savidge. "You," he spat out. "What the hell are you—"

"What are you doing here?" Lyssa countered, needing to nip the head of steam she could see building in George.

"Now we know why your Mom didn't answer her phone," George said in a falsely saccharine tone of voice. "She must have been really busy. Or distracted."

"It hasn't rung in the half hour I've been here," Savidge interjected, obviously trying to defuse the situation.

"I started trying to call you from Jessie's cell phone when we got off the Thruway, like five or six times. It rang and rang. You didn't pick up and the answering machine didn't kick in. She lives in Princeton and she's allowed to have her Mustang at school, so she dropped me off at the train station there. I had to wait until it pulled into 30th Street Station to call from a pay phone. When you *still* didn't answer, I panicked and called Dad."

"Well, I'm sorry you had so much trouble, sweetie, but I didn't know you were coming home this weekend."

She glared at Savidge. "Obviously."

"You must be Michelle." Savidge stepped forward and thrust out his hand. "My name is Robert Savidge. I'm one of the attorneys from the firm that administers your trust fund."

Michelle's demeanor changed at once. "Attorney? Mom, is something wrong?"

"Not at all," Savidge said smoothly. "Like you, I couldn't reach Mrs. Markham by phone. That overnight case, George—" he turned his attention to the older man with a bland look on his face, " — is mine. I spent the past week in London, so was basically out of touch with my office. I had the cab drop me off here, since it's on my way home."

He paused, lifting an eyebrow as he skewered George with a laser stare. "I just wanted to make sure that the transfer of funds from the trust to the college had occurred, since there was some minor glitch."

George made a blustering sound, but it was obvious he didn't want to get into a pissing contest with this particular attorney about Michelle's trust fund. He turned as if to go stalking down the hall, but stopped as his gaze settled on the broken shards of china scattered on the floor. "What the hell happened here?"

"A noise startled Mrs. Markham and the cup fell out of her hand. It sounded like metal scraping on metal. She thought someone was trying to break in, but of course it turned out to be a house key. Her car must be in the garage, because I didn't see it when the cab dropped me off. So it would be natural for a burglar to assume no one was home."

"That's right," Lyssa said, grateful for Savidge's lawyerly ability to think on his feet. "It never occurred to me that it might be you."

Then her motherly instincts belatedly kicked in. "You must be exhausted, honey. Would you like me to make you some hot cocoa? I straightened up your room when I came back from New Hampshire, so the sheets are clean."

"Well, it seems like all's right with the world," Savidge said. "It was a pleasure meeting you, Michelle. Don't worry about your trust fund. It's in good hands.

George, would you mind giving me a lift home? I only live in the next town."

George glared at the attorney with *over my dead body* written all over his face. Savidge absorbed his withering stare with nonchalance.

Michelle was eyeing Savidge speculatively. *Oh, God,* Lyssa thought, *don't let her realize that there's something between us.* A quick glance at his crotch assured her that his hard-on had dissipated, but she couldn't help wondering if Michelle had noticed it when she first came into the kitchen.

"My ride isn't going back until Labor Day," Michelle said, still looking at him. "So I'll be here all day tomorrow. Would it be possible, Mr. Savidge, since this trust fund is for my benefit, do you think maybe I could get a copy of it and you can go over it with me? After all, I *am* emancipated, right? Since I'm eighteen and living away from home?"

"Now, Michelle, don't get your pretty little head in a tizzy. You don't need to—"

"Oh, knock it off, Dad. Maybe you could browbeat Mom with that 'Don't worry about it, you belong in the kitchen' crap from the 1950s, but this is me you're talking to. I want to know. I have a *right* to know about something that impacts my future."

She turned back to Savidge with an ingenuous smile. "Would it be possible to meet at your office tomorrow afternoon to explain the provisions of the trust to me?"

Lyssa gave her daughter a dark look. "Michelle, you can't ask him to give up his Sunday. He just spent a long week in London on business. The poor man must be exhausted with jet lag."

"On the contrary. It would be my pleasure." Savidge came to stand next to Lyssa. "I plan on seeing a lot of your mother in the future, Michelle. I look forward to getting to know you—both of you—better." He bent down to press his lips to Lyssa's temple. "But you're right, I'm almost dead on my feet. George?"

"You—you—how dare you?" Throwing one last baleful glare at Savidge, George spun on his heel. "Call a cab. I have a brand-new wife waiting for me at home."

But Lyssa barely heard him. Her mind was still trying to assimilate what Savidge had just publicly announced. *He wants to get to know us better. Us. Meaning both Michelle and me.* Her face must have reflected her astonishment, because she became vaguely aware of Michelle's fingers gripping her arm.

"Mom? Are you all right?"

Lyssa came out of her stupor just in time to hear the front door slam hard enough to rattle the mirror hanging in the hallway.

"Mom, it's okay. I knew as soon as I saw the two of you that you weren't just attorney and client."

Still speechless, Lyssa could feel her cheeks burning.

"It's okay," Michelle repeated. "You deserve a life, too. I wasn't cool with Dad getting married like that, without telling me, but truth?" She glanced at Savidge, then lowered her voice to whisper in Lyssa's ear. "You made out a lot better than he did."

Lyssa couldn't help it. She burst out laughing then wrapped her arms around her daughter. "Oh, 'Chelle, you're precious! I love you, you know that?"

"Love you too, Mom." She returned the hug. "But I'm really tired. I'll take a rain check on that cocoa." She yawned flamboyantly, as if to reinforce her statement. "Why don't *you* drive him home?"

"I can call a cab—" Savidge started to say.

"Mom." She stepped back and gave Lyssa a meaningful stare. "I'm planning to sleep really, really late tomorrow. So you take it easy on the road and drive real slow, y'hear?"

Turning to Savidge, she said, "I'm so tired I probably won't wake up until noon. Then Mom and I can have brunch and maybe Mom can bring me to your office at, say, three o'clock? Would that be okay with you?"

He favored Michelle with one of his lopsided, Harrison Ford smiles. "If you decide to study law, young lady, I'd be glad to sponsor you for an internship at Quick, Bowers & Savidge. For now, good night and sleep tight."

"I know, don't let the bedbugs bite. See you tomorrow afternoon."

She got halfway down the hall before she turned and said, "Mom? You can come up in a few minutes and tuck me in, okay?"

"Okay," Lyssa said faintly.

Listening to her daughter's footsteps fade up the carpeted stairs, Lyssa sighed. "She's all grown up, isn't she?"

"Children have a way of doing that." Savidge came to stand beside her, slung an arm around her shoulder and pulled her close. "You did a good job with her."

Lyssa just shook her head in disbelief. "She knows."

"At least she's older than I was when I realized my dad still had sex at the decrepit old age of forty."

A few minutes later, when she heard the toilet flush and the board creak in the upstairs hallway, Lyssa knew she had to face the inevitable grilling. She took the stairs rather apprehensively, wondering what kind of lecture she'd be receiving from her daughter.

She needn't have worried.

"Mom, he's a hunkster! Where'd you find him?"

Lyssa's heart skipped a beat. She wouldn't, *couldn't* tell her about the masquerade. Then she remembered. "The law firm. The trust's regular lawyer was tied up in court all week, so Savidge stepped in. They needed some extra paperwork signed. Your father was on his honeymoon and not reachable, so they called me."

Michelle snuggled under the flowered sheet. "And the rest, as they say, is history, right?"

A smile tugged at the corners of Lyssa's mouth. "We'll see about that."

"Mom, you were making out, weren't you? And we interrupted you."

"That's none of your—"

"I could tell. You haven't looked that, well, *rosy* in a long time. And he looks like a great kisser." She giggled. "Is he? Come on, now, dish!"

"Don't be impertinent. Things will unfold at their own pace. When and if it's time to inform you of anything, I will."

Michelle sighed. "You know, I really love Daddy, but he treated you rotten the last couple of years. I hate to say it, but you look much happier now than you did when he left." She rolled her eyes. "And for that—that, good Lord, she's not much older than I am! And too skinny by half. She looks anorexic. I hope he starts feeding her."

"Your father and I just grew in different directions. Now, I really have to go. Savidge is probably asleep in the front hall."

Eyes drowsing, Michelle murmured, "Mom? Why do you call him by his last name?"

Startled at the question, Lyssa said, "I don't know. It just seemed — appropriate."

"You mean, he's 'savage'?" She giggled again, a dreamy smile on her face.

"That's enough, young lady. You may be emancipated, but when you're in my house, you still have to listen to your mother. Go to sleep now." Lyssa hoped her voice was authoritative enough to forestall any more such awkward questions. She tiptoed out of the room, closed the door quietly, and went to find her savage.

Chapter Fourteen

Unhurried, exquisite friction. He lay behind her, both of them on their sides, tucked together like two spoons in a tray. Her head rested on his outstretched arm, with his other he gripped her hip. His cock was sliding in and out of her cunt with agonizing, tantalizing deliberation, like a film running in slow motion to give the viewer ample time to recognize and appreciate that she was being well and truly fucked by a master.

Lyssa smiled inwardly as she watched the delicious dream unfold on the screen of her subconscious. Savidge had made a valiant effort to continue what they'd started in the kitchen before their interruption, but as soon as they undressed and fell into his massive bed, he'd pulled her into his arms and succumbed to jet lag. Lyssa snuggled into him and allowed herself to relax into sleep as well.

With Michelle's blessing resonating in her mind, her dream-self conjured up a fitting scenario to complete the coupling they'd started in her kitchen, to allow Lyssa the pleasure of bringing Savidge to his own release. Every leisurely stroke of his cock seemed to lift her passion higher, sending erotic shock waves through her womb and down into every microscopic nerve ending in her body.

She arched her back so as to press her hips more firmly into his, signaling her desire and impatience for him to increase the tempo of his thrusts. Maddeningly, he didn't take the hint, but kept sliding, sliding into her pussy with infinite precision, withdrawing to the very tip of his hot cock, then slowly pushing his thick length back in until she could feel his balls tight against her thighs.

Heat scorched her back, her ass cheeks. Fingers of pressure dug into the soft flesh of her hip. Puffs of warm air tickled the fine, soft hairs at her nape.

Lyssa's breathing roughened. She felt caught in one of those dream sequences she'd experienced in the past, as if she was running from — or maybe to — something, but inexplicably stayed rooted to the spot, unable to stir. She needed to pump her hips, to *move*, to make him quicken his strokes, or she'd go insane with wanting. But she discovered that her hips were caught in a vise, her legs held hostage between two solid lengths of supple pipe that held her immobile.

The arm supporting her head moved, cradling her more firmly to the heat of his chest. She felt a tug on her nipple. The incredible sensations rocketing through her almost made her come right then and there. She struggled to wake up from the dream — the feelings she was experiencing were too scorching to be only half-remembered in the light of day. She needed to masturbate herself to climax, because the dream was much too vivid and yet, somehow, unfulfilling, because the dream Savidge refused to speed up the tempo of his fucking, something the real Savidge would never countenance, knowing the way he'd always fucked her with abandon.

Her eyelids fluttered open. The darkness was alleviated by the soft silver light of moonglow through an uncurtained window. The heat—

The heat at her back continued unabated.

So did the measured stroking between her cunt lips.

So did the sharp tugging on her nipple.

"*Savidge!*" she rasped. "What are you doing?"

A low chuckle rumbled in his chest, vibrating through her very bones. "What does it feel like I'm doing?"

"I thought—I thought I dreamt that we—"

"Were fucking?" The question was punctuated by another leisurely movement of his cock, making her vividly aware of how aroused, how slick and wet she was, how much she wanted his thrusts to be more forceful.

She felt, as well, the firm grip of his hand on her hip, became aware that her legs were held captive by his. Became aware that she was sheened with a film of perspiration and that her entire body was erotically charged.

"But you fell asleep—"

"A few hours was enough to refresh me, but by damn, I couldn't wait for the sun to wake you, not when you were in my arms and making my cock as hard as a boulder. I had to be inside you, to give you what we both want. It felt so good just to hold you close, to slip it in and out while you were sleeping."

"How—how long have you...?"

He lifted his head and nipped at her earlobe from behind, gave another leisurely stroke. "Long enough to go crazy with wanting you."

"But you have me," she countered logically, wiggling her ass into him as much in desperation as in suggestion.

"Now I do," he murmured. "I had to wait for you to wake up before I..."

He slammed into her. A feral cry ripped from her throat. "Yes!"

It was as though that single word opened the floodgates. Savidge began pumping into her with a vengeance bordering on frenzy. Lyssa braced herself against his onslaught, welcoming his savage thrusts. She reached an arm across his hip to his ass cheeks. With his thighs spread to clamp around hers, she had easy access to his balls. She squeezed them, molded them, reveling in how tight they were up against the base of his cock. She felt, heard their distinctive slap as they pounded into her flesh every time he moved.

With a visceral cry that sounded as though it emanated from the very core of him, Savidge climaxed, shooting his juices into her in one pulsation after another. In seconds, Lyssa joined him in an earthquake that triggered aftershocks for several minutes before she could think coherently.

Many moments later, when his breathing had finally changed from harsh panting to slow, even breaths, he managed to say, "I'm glad you woke up when you did. I don't think I could have waited another minute."

He kissed her shoulder, then eased back away from her. "Good thing I used a super-large condom. My body must have spent the whole week manufacturing my cum. Probably because all I did was think of you. And this."

Totally boneless and replete, Lyssa felt her mouth stretch into a Cheshire cat smile. She wanted to tell him what a mind-blowing experience it had been, but she simply hadn't an atom of energy left. All she could do was purr.

She felt the mattress shift as he presumably discarded the used condom. Then he returned to mold himself to her curves. They lay for an interval in delicious, sleepy silence, Savidge's arms around her, Lyssa's back pressed into him.

In a half-dream state, she realized that of all the explosive times they'd had sex, this was the first time they'd actually spent the night together. It felt so peaceful, so *right* to be sharing his bed.

He stirred. "I still haven't given you the gift I brought you from London."

She turned in the circle of his arms. "This is the best present you could've given me." The hint of moonlight through the uncurtained window gave him a ghostly look, all angles and shadows except for pinpoints of light in his dark eyes.

Kissing the tip of her nose, he said, "Me, too. But I still want to give you this." He turned to his side of the bed and flicked on the lamp, which gave off a soft, dim light akin to a candle's glow. She felt the bed tilt slightly as he reached inside a drawer of the nightstand.

"Here. I had it specially made at Harrod's."

"Savidge. You don't have to—"

"I do, and I did. Open it." Sitting up, he held out a silver-wrapped package about two inches square and an inch thick. A lapel pin, maybe.

At least it isn't an engagement ring, she thought, remembering his declaration to Michelle about getting to know both of them better. She wasn't ready for a commitment after her rotten experience with her ex. She'd just found her sexuality, her freedom, and didn't want to be subservient to any man, even one as luscious as this one.

She scooted up to the top of the bed, fluffing her pillow at her back, and settled her attention on the box. The sheet lay crumpled at her waist, leaving her breasts bare to his scrutiny, but she discovered she'd lost her inhibitions about her body, thanks to Savidge—and the men of the Platinum Society, she silently added.

Unwrapping the silver paper, she opened the box. Nestled inside a black velvet bed lay—a ring. With a catch in her throat, she picked it up, inspected it. The silvery band was intricately engraved.

"Oh. Just like my new bracelet."

His gaze on her was tender. "Right down to your initials."

Lyssa tipped up the ring. The *LMM* winked at her in the soft light. And reminded her of the bracelet she'd found under his sofa cushion. With the initials *CYS*. Columba Yount Savidge.

She would *not* give in to curiosity. To jealousy. To ask about his relationship with his former wife.

"Do you still see your wife?" she blurted out anyway.

Savidge stiffened beside her. "Ex-wife. What the heck made you think of her?"

Lyssa ducked her head. "I'm sorry, I just—the initials—they reminded me of the bracelet I found in your living room."

"Because…?" Savidge raised an eyebrow in inquiry.

Sorry she'd opened her stupid mouth, Lyssa squirmed under his intense look. "CYS. Aren't those her initials?"

"Yes, but if you've looked through the roster, you'd know that Columba isn't a member of the Platinum Society, so she wouldn't have had a bracelet. She was more interested in money than in sex."

Marginally mollified by his comment, Lyssa resisted the urge to ask whose it was. She'd already ruined the cozy mood his surprise gift had created. Closing her grip around the ring within her palm, she edged away from him with another apology on her lips.

He reached out to grab her arm and pulled her close to him. Off balance, she came to rest diagonally across his naked chest as he asked, "Is that a note of jealousy I detect in this line of questioning?"

"I—maybe." There. She'd said it. After all, he admitted being jealous when she'd teased him about his father being a good kisser.

"I think I know who owns that bracelet."

"Who?"

"Yuki."

"Your cook? But the initials are C—"

"I know, CYS. But Yuki is thoroughly Japanese. He still writes his name in the Asian style, with the surname first. Chiba Yuki Santoro. CYS. I'm sure he requested it that way."

Her heart unaccountably soaring at the answer to the riddle, she snuggled against him. "You won't punish him, will you? For doing—things—on your sofa while you're traveling?"

A deep chuckle reverberated through his chest. "Won't even mention it. If you want me to, I can just put it in some unobtrusive place where he'll find it."

"Sounds good. But weren't you even a little curious whose it was when I told you over the phone? You just said 'Finders, keepers' like it wasn't a big deal."

He shrugged. "I've hosted a Society affair or two. It could have been anyone's. But we've gotten off the subject here." He tunneled his fingers through her disheveled hair and gifted her with a long, leisurely kiss that had her toes curling. When they broke, both were breathing more heavily and she was lying more or less on top of him, half tangled in the sheets.

"The ring," he murmured against her temple. "You could wear it on your index finger."

She pushed herself up on her elbows to look into his eyes, the ring feeling warm and alive in her closed palm.

"I'd like you to wear it any time you go to the Platinum Society," he continued, "to remind you of me. I'm not insisting on an exclusive relationship. I know you're just discovering your sensuality and would like to explore what you want out of yourself, out of life."

He tucked a tendril of blonde hair behind her ear. "But before you choose to fuck another man, I would ask you to look at this ring on your finger, remember the man who gave it to you, and go from there. I won't stand in the way of anything you want to do. I just want you to make a conscious decision."

Lyssa could feel tears stinging the backs of her eyes. He understood her better than she understood herself. She blinked several times before she was able to lift her gaze to his.

The look on his face almost undid her. Tender, passionate, little-boy-insecure. *Vulnerable.* A word she'd never before associated with Savidge.

Could it be that she really meant something to him?

She could barely swallow around the lump in her throat.

"Savidge." His name ripped from deep inside her. She lifted herself off him and sat up. Clumsily she fitted the ring onto her left index finger, as he'd suggested, even though her first thought was to wear it on her ring finger.

Then she turned to him, arms open to welcome him. They met in a crushing bear hug in the middle of the bed, in the middle of the night, in the middle of the life-changing experience that Savidge had wrought in her.

"Will you let me help you explore the possibilities?"

Lyssa drew back from his embrace just enough to see the intensity of his gaze. His pupils were so dilated that only the merest hint of their chocolate-brown color showed in his irises. She felt like she was being drawn into their endless depths and hadn't the slightest desire to be rescued.

"Isn't that what you've been doing?" Her lips quirked up in a coquettish smile. "In front of an audience of masked, naked revelers? On a desk in a Philadelphia lawyer's office? In a corporate bathroom high above Billy Penn's statue? Scalding phone sex? None of which, I assure you, had even occurred to me before I met you."

He tightened his hold around her shoulders, a movement which shifted his awakening cock to press against her thigh. "That's only the beginning. Do you remember the Indian brave tied to the table? The man handcuffed to the ceiling?"

Lyssa's breath hitched. Did she ever. She also remembered wondering how it would feel to be captive, to be teased and dominated by someone who would bring her to the brink time after time and not allow her any release. Her insides tightened in anticipation—and anxiety. Deep down she knew he wouldn't hurt her. Hadn't he watched out for the guests as majordomo? Still, to be totally helpless before him...

"Let me show you what they experienced. Submit to my will."

Did she dare? Did she really, *really* trust him?

"Let me make you truly free."

Yes. She trusted him, wanted to experience everything he could teach her. Taking a deep breath, she said, "Show me how."

The next thing she knew, the sheet had been tugged to the foot of the bed and she was flat on her back, trapped under the sinew and muscle of a man who was all heat and arousal. Slowly, deliberately, he pulled both her arms up over her head so she was stretched out as though on a rack, then reached over to the nightstand again and retrieved an object that tinkled metallically. She felt something cold encasing one wrist, then the other.

Instinctively she jerked her arms. They didn't budge.

With a satanic grin, Savidge rolled off her and, nudging her legs wide apart, knelt between them. "You're in my power now," he growled.

Handcuffs. She twisted her head to catch a glimpse of the headboard. He'd slipped the chain around a spindle so she was helpless to move. She could feel their cold bite on her heated skin, the pressure of hard metal against soft tissue.

For a moment he just knelt there, his gaze avidly roaming her exposed flesh, all soft shadows and luminous highlights from the bedside lamp. Gooseflesh prickled wherever his gaze touched her.

He leaned forward, licked a path on the outer edge of her cunt lips, then blew soft puffs of air on the moistened skin. Bolts of electricity shot through Lyssa.

Savidge laved the other side, adding a nip here and there during his leisurely path.

Unconsciously, Lyssa lifted her hips to follow his mouth, but he moved just out of range.

"Uh-unh. I have not given you permission to move." With an open palm, he slapped the fleshiest part of her hip in reproach.

Lyssa's eyes widened, but she said nothing, just concentrated on breathing normally. She would *not* beg.

His big hands grazed cloud-soft down her sensitive inner thighs until he reached her knees, then stroked their way back up, up toward the nub that throbbed with the need for his tongue, his hand...

And stopped inches away. Hovered. Teased her with its nearness.

She waited, silently begging with a hungry look in her eyes, but staying motionless.

"Good girl." He moistened his index finger with saliva and feathered a touch up and down her exposed slit.

A moan escaped her, she couldn't help it. She was wet and ready again. The sight of his cock, hanging hard and thick between his thighs, made her lick her lips. She devoured it with her eyes, the strong, purple vein running from the thicket of black hair to the crown, the pearly drop at its tip.

She drew her legs together until they were embracing Savidge's knees.

With a swiftness that made her blink, he grabbed her ankles and pulled her legs up high enough that her knees touched her chest, exposing the backs of her thighs as well as her ass cheeks pulled tight against her pelvic bones. And slapped her with more force than before, first on one thigh, then the other, then down to her ass, one whack on each cheek.

"I told you not to move."

Over her bent knees, Lyssa gauged his expression. He wouldn't *really* hurt her. Would he? She decided silence, stillness were called for.

Especially since her skin tingled wherever his palm had smacked her.

"You should see your skin. It's as red as—" and he ran a finger across her cunt lips again "—as this."

Lyssa felt her inner muscles contract in an involuntary desire to have his finger, his cock, his tongue, *anything*, inside her.

"Poor, abused skin," he murmured, strewing moist kisses on every inch of skin that he'd stung with his palm. He licked, stroked, took little nips with his teeth, circling in ever-narrowing spirals until he was licking her cunt lips again. Still he gripped her ankles with one strong hand, holding her legs immobile, but no other part of him touched her except for his mouth.

Lyssa bit the inside of her cheek. Need was building in her, hot lava coursing through her veins and getting ready to erupt. She hadn't had nearly enough of his cock when he'd wakened her with his deliberately slow fucking. She'd come so quickly because she'd been without him for too long, and she was primed for an encore.

"Savidge," she pleaded.

Smack! "You disobey me again, wench? When I ordered you not to move, that included moving your lips. Do you want me to leave without…"

A whimper escaped her, a cross between a sob and a sigh. She didn't need him to finish the sentence. He wouldn't, *couldn't* leave. She needed him to fuck her, right now!

After another slow, thorough traversing of his tongue on the newest red mark on her ass, Savidge gently brought her legs down to rest on the sheet. Perspiration had accumulated where her thighs had pressed against her calves, and the shock of the cool sheet under her skin contrasted with the furnace within.

Savidge positioned himself to straddle her, his knees aligned with her breasts. His cock, rampant now and pointing its thick, dark crown to the headboard, was tantalizingly close. If she lifted her head a little, she could capture it in her mouth. If he refused to stick it in her cunt, she knew she could still derive enormous pleasure by sucking him.

But she dare not. If she disobeyed, perhaps he *would* leave without satisfying her.

His eyes glittered as he loomed over her. He bent forward and gripped the headboard, forming a triangle — she the base, the headboard on a vertical, and Savidge the angle. The exact angle to position his cock a few inches from her mouth.

"Don't think about moving." His voice was a hoarse rasp.

Dipping his torso, he trailed the tip of his cock across her face. Lyssa felt her eyes cross as she followed its motion. So close. So tantalizingly close she wanted to swallow it, bite it, suck it dry. Instead, she held back, although she couldn't control the way her breathing had accelerated. Her breasts rose and fell noticeably; her arms trembled with the need to hold him.

"Open your mouth, wench, and take your punishment."

On a groan, Lyssa obeyed, capturing his cock with a desperate eagerness she couldn't control. Hot steel assaulted the warm recesses of her mouth. She lifted her head to take all of him, but her lips only came up halfway, he was so big. She drew him in, retreated, rolled her tongue around the ridge of its head.

He hissed, and began to move his hips to fuck her mouth. She tensed her cheek muscles to offer resistance as he pushed in, let her teeth scrape his skin as he withdrew.

And again. And yet again. She had a hard time breathing, her mouth was so full of him. Her heart was pounding, the blood surging to her cunt in yearning. Her arms ached from trying to free herself so she could touch him, hold him. She could feel the coarse hairs of his legs as he moved them closer to her body in a kind of embrace.

She lifted her gaze to him. He was watching her intently, his expression one of utter possession and mastery.

Suddenly he pushed back from the headboard, his cock slipping out of her mouth with a wet popping sound, and clambered over her leg. In a swift motion, he flipped her over onto her belly. The cuffs clanked as the chain criss-crossed in the spin.

His strong hands gripped her hips and lifted them up until her knees were more or less centered under her. She scrambled to brace herself on her hands.

"Not like that." He pressed a palm between her shoulder blades. "On your elbows."

She complied, aware that the movement made her ass stick up even higher, as if in offering. He paused a moment, his breath coming in harsh pants.

"Spread your legs, wench."

She did, then with a rough nudge from his hands, her knees moved even farther apart. His hands tightened their grip on her hips. He spread her ass cheeks until she was sure he could see all of her, from the cunt lips and the moist passage between them, to her other opening that had never before been exposed to another's scrutiny.

Then...nothing.

Oh God, he was torturing her. She didn't even have the pleasure of looking at him; she couldn't see him when she turned her head to glance over her shoulder. If he didn't fuck her soon, she'd *die*. It was as though every synapse, every nerve ending had gravitated to the core of her and was on fire. A fire that could be extinguished only if he pumped enough juice into her.

She felt totally exposed, totally at his mercy, with her ass high in the air, blonde hair flowing around her face like a curtain to pool on the mattress, wrists shackled, legs spread wide almost to the point of discomfort. Her breasts hung unfettered, swaying with every gasping breath she was able to manage. Still, she was expectant, eager. Behind her, he remained still as a sphinx.

"*Savidge!*"

Her raw, undisciplined cry was immediately answered with a resounding smack against her ass.

"Please," she whined, "I need—" *Smack!*

"Silence!"

"Savidge, don't tease me, I can't stand it any more. I need you in me!"

"I will teach you to wait, my love." He pitched his voice low, the vibrant rumble echoing within her very bones, kicking her desperate passion up another notch. "Don't fight me on this. Don't think about the destination. Just enjoy the journey. Give up your will to me."

"Please…"

"Lyssa." Sharp with command. "I forbid you to speak."

Lyssa's breath hitched. Their previous couplings flashed through her mind. Their first encounter, with her naked and writhing in full view of a dozen people. The frenzied way he fucked her on his desk. The bathroom threesome, where he had the presence of mind to pull out when he remembered the missing condom. The taste, the feel of his cock in her mouth when he climaxed all too soon. The sweet, rocking possession from behind just a short while ago, the most delicious awakening from sleep she'd ever experienced.

Why didn't he want to fuck her now, when she was so primed? When *he* was hard as a ship's mast?

She felt the mattress dip, then spring back as though he'd gotten off. *No!* He couldn't leave her like this!

"Don't move."

He came into her vision then, standing at the side of the bed, gloriously virile and male, his cock rampant, a length of white silk in his hand. "Recognize this? It's one of Salome's veils. The last one she discarded. The one that covered the most exquisite pussy I've ever seen. This veil holds fond memories for me."

A lump formed in Lyssa's throat. Was he really that sentimental to have saved it?

Leaning across to the center of the bed, he wrapped the veil around her eyes and tied it at the back of her head.

"Now all you can do is *feel*." She felt his lips graze her cheek. "Let yourself go."

That tender kiss broke her resistance. With her sight gone, she concentrated on her other senses. The lingering, slightly salty taste of his cock in her mouth. The scent of her cunt juices, of his aroused male smell. The luxurious feel of the sheet under her knees, elbows, forearms. The way her fingers and toes dug into the soft layer of cushion overlaying the firmness of the mattress. The harsh rasp of his heavy breathing, her own quick, short breaths.

The rough texture of his—tongue?—running up the curve of her slit. To Lyssa it felt as though he had touched every single nerve ending between her legs.

She arched her back like a cat, offering herself to his mouth. He growled then dipped his tongue between the folds of her cunt lips. A hint of stubble lightly scratched the insides of her ass cheeks as he moved his tongue up and down, laving her slit. His fingers felt like feathers as they stroked her inner thighs, drawing abstract designs on her tingling skin.

Whimpering with the need to climax, she forced herself to relax and simply enjoy, letting the sensations flow over her like warm summer rain.

A long finger looped round and round, circling ever closer to her clit. When he finally touched it, a mewling sound escaped her. She wiggled her hips, needing more, begging without words.

He chuckled deep in his throat then tormented her with short, teasing strokes of that finger on her clit in between endless seconds of waiting.

"Savidge, please!"

At last, at last, the glorious feel of a finger or two inside her, his thumb resting at the top of her crack, at the entrance to her asshole. He reached an arm around her hip to caress her clit, gradually rubbing it harder while he began finger-fucking her. His teeth took nips of her skin at her hip, her waist, her back, all the while bringing her to a higher and higher pitch.

She could feel the sexual lava bubbling to the surface of her consciousness, her vagina contracting, her cunt oozing juices. More frenetic now, she wiggled her ass in counterpoint to the motion of his fingers, felt his thumb pressing into her asshole.

The volcano blew. She felt every muscle go rigid as fiery sensations exploded across her body, from the center outward. She let out a long, incoherent moan that came from the visceral core of her being.

Before she had time to take a gasping breath, she felt his cock shove hard into her cunt again and again, heard the slapping sound of moist skin against moist skin, and she climaxed again. Still he kept thrusting, his fingers digging into her hips as he pounded into her. She pushed backward into him, wanting more and harder, and he gave it to her, holding nothing back. Her breasts jolted back and forth viciously with each impact. Her hair swung in wild abandon as she tossed her head about.

He slowed his rhythm, his strokes becoming less frantic. *No!* she wanted to shout. She wanted it as fast, as brutal as he could give it to her; she knew she was more than a match for his ferocity.

"Go with the flow," he murmured, as though he'd read her mind.

Obeying, she concentrated on the feel of each stroke as he slid the hard, burning cock into her slick passage, then pulled out oh-so-slowly. Felt the tug on one breast as he rolled the nipple between his fingertips. Felt the dribble of her juices down her leg, the bead of sweat rolling down her temple to disappear into the silken blindfold. Inhaled the intoxicating smell of sex in the air.

Felt the shock of his finger, strangely cool, slipping into her asshole.

She tensed, tightening up the opening. "Savidge, I don't think…"

"Shh, it's all right. I put a lot of lube on my finger."

He continued leisurely moving his cock in and out of her cunt, then gradually began to move his finger in a similar rhythm in and out of her asshole. The sensation of the latter was different, but most pleasurable, she decided. As she relaxed into the moment, she felt her breathing quicken, and realized she was making those little purring sounds in her throat again.

Savidge stepped up his tempo in both orifices. She pushed into him, glorying in the new, delicious sensations he was evoking. Suddenly she felt his cock withdraw from her cunt. His hands grabbed her hips in a vise-like grip and she felt him seeking entrance to her asshole. "You're so wet, my cock is covered with your sweet juice," he murmured. "I promise, it won't hurt. Do you trust me?"

"Yes," she gasped.

He pushed slowly, slowly. She tensed again, aware of pressure bordering on pain.

"Relax, love. Let it happen."

He released his death grip on her hips. She felt him drawing his fingers across her hips, her ass cheeks, down the sensitive backs of her thighs. With one finger, he drew designs on her skin, as though he was writing.

Concentrating, she deciphered the letters. M-i-n-e.

With a Cheshire cat smile on her face that he couldn't see, she did relax then, allowing his cock to penetrate further, and slowly further, until the hair surrounding the base of his cock tickled her skin.

He leaned forward, cupping her breasts in his hands, and whispered her name. His palms were damp, his breathing a harsh rasp. He kissed her shoulder, then bit into the fleshy part with his teeth, hard enough to make her cry out.

Then he was moving again, in and out of her asshole, making her forget that flash of pain from his teeth and overwhelming her with a whole new series of sensations. With his hands clamped onto her hips again, the pounding escalated, sending her spiraling higher and higher, her legs trembling so hard she could barely stay in place, until she screamed his name over and over and felt his semen pulsing into her anal passage in hot gushes.

In that moment, Lyssa understood the meaning of freedom.

Epilogue

"Congratulations. You just sold another painting."

"Oh, Kat, really? Which one?"

"That little close-up of a rose unfolding that looks like a cunt."

Lyssa glanced quickly around the alcove where the two friends stood, hoping no one had overheard Kat's comment. Sure, she and Savidge used such terms whenever they made love, which was almost every day when he wasn't traveling, but here in Kat's art gallery, on the opening-night cocktail party of her first solo show, Lyssa wasn't sure it was appropriate.

She sipped Cristal from a champagne glass, savoring the moment. Kat had told her she could have sold "The Oasis" several times—and at a five-figure sticker price, no less—but Lyssa refused to part with it. She was planning to give it to Savidge as a Christmas present. After all, he'd been the catalyst that awakened the sensuality in her painting as well as in her mind and body. He was the panther that lapped at the abstract nude within the shimmering water. He was the man who could weaken her knees with just a glance.

As he was doing now, wending his way across the crowded gallery, greeting friends as they stopped him, but always reconnecting his gaze with hers while skillfully moving on after only a few words.

Lyssa thought she'd never tire of looking at him. Not only was he drop-dead handsome, the man oozed presence. He commanded a room just by entering it. His intense concentration directed at a person made them feel they were the only important thing in his world at that moment.

He stopped at Lyssa's side, encircled her shoulder with his arm, and kissed her on the cheek. "Congratulations. The buzz I hear is that the artist will be an overnight sensation. Another Georgia O'Keeffe or Frida Kahlo."

Eyes sparkling, Lyssa raised her face to him. "I never dreamed other people would see so much merit in my painting. It started as just something to vent my frustrations on."

"And became a barometer for other things as well," Kat chimed in.

"Mmm. 'The Oasis,' you mean?" Eyes warm, Savidge stroked Lyssa's cheek with a knuckle. "Kat told me the timing of that painting."

Lyssa stilled. She didn't quite take offense, because she'd learned to go with the flow in the two months she and Savidge had been getting to know each other. Still, it rankled that Kat was so free with information that was, if not confidential, then certainly private.

"I'm honored to have played a part in nurturing your artistic sensibilities. There's a freedom in your latest works, the brush strokes more sure, more vibrant, that's missing in the early paintings."

"Two different periods in my life."

"They're still sensuous, the early ones," Kat said. "It's just the subject matter that's different."

"I should take more business trips." Savidge chuckled. "Every time I return, you've completed another canvas. Each one better than the last."

Lyssa sipped, looking at him over the rim of her glass. "I have lots of inspiration."

"Oh my God." Kat raised her hand to her breast. "He came."

"Who?"

Kat lobbed a self-satisfied smile at Lyssa. "Simms. I emailed him a .tif file of the reclining nude."

"Who is he?"

"Only the most prestigious private art collector in New York City, that's who. If he buys, you've made the big time. Excuse me while I go make nice with him." She winked. "I feel a sale coming on. And I think the prices just doubled."

Lyssa watched the gallery owner weave through the crowd—a crowd she'd gathered to showcase her friend's work—stopping to chat or answer questions, adroitly making a circuit of the room while not appearing to be heading for her target. A feeling of well-being stole over her. She had come a long way since Kat convinced her to walk into a costume ball wearing seven veils and a mask. She had found herself. And she had the pleasure of Savidge's company.

Could life get any better?

* * * * *

"I found it, Savidge! I found the absolutely perfect home for you."

It had been more than a week since her triumphant entry into the art world. Two articles in the local newspapers, a total of four paintings sold — the New York art collector had indeed purchased the reclining nude — and several offers to buy "The Oasis". Lyssa's head spun every time she thought about it.

Unfortunately, her art was still a hobby. Selling real estate was her bread and butter. And she'd worked damn hard to find exactly what he'd asked for — a smaller, less ostentatious home than the mansion she'd just found a buyer for. His requirements included a large yard, mature trees and landscaping, a bedroom big enough for his huge bed and two armoires, a professional kitchen, multi-bay garage, and a good-sized studio.

"Great! I'm free in an hour. I'll meet you at your office."

He picked her up in the Porsche Boxster, saying he'd met with a client who had several vintage Porsches and he wanted to "speak the same language". Although his Aston Martin was much roomier, Lyssa enjoyed the feeling of carefree abandon as she sat low to the ground in the sports car that he handled like a racecar driver.

Following her direction, he pulled into a driveway between two square brick pillars on a quiet street in upscale Wayne and stopped under a porte-cochere at one side of the Tudor, brick-and-timbered home with an interesting intersection of rooflines. She opened the lockbox, retrieved the key and unlocked the front door.

"Best of all, it's in move-in condition. The owners upgraded everything in the past few years — new roof, wiring, all the bathrooms, wood floors throughout, all refinished. And wait until you see the kitchen! All the appliances are top-of-the-line. Sub Zero fridge, Wolf dual-fuel pro range, walk-in pantry, loads of built-ins."

When she showed Savidge the room in question, he stopped in the doorway and just drank it all in. "Yuki will love it." Then a slow smile spread across his face. He turned to her. "Maybe you need a kitchen like this. To encourage you to be a better cook."

She gave him a look of mock outrage. "You mean you don't like my roast octopus with avocado and chocolate stuffing?"

"I like it fine. I like the cook even better."

He nimbly took her attention off the implied slur with a burning kiss against the pantry door. When she could catch her breath, she set her mind against being sidetracked again and showed him the rest of the house. He approved of everything—the living room with its parquet floor and tiled fireplace, spacious library with bookshelves on two walls, dining room overlooking a large patio, guest room and bath in a secluded downstairs corner overlooking the garden, and upstairs, a roomy master bedroom with two huge walk-in closets, whirlpool tub in the master bath, three smaller bedrooms, large compartmented bath, and a laundry room right where most of the dirty laundry accumulates.

At the far end of the hall, she took him down a half flight of steps. "Here's the *piece de resistance*. This room is over the garage. You probably noticed on the way in, there are four bays. It also has an inside stairway near the back entrance."

She opened the door. Light poured into the huge room from two skylights and an entire wall of north-facing windows. Walking to one of those windows, she gestured to the outside. "Look at the view! You can see the design of the garden. It's like wedges and spokes radiating out from the gazebo."

When he didn't respond, she turned around with a questioning gaze.

Savidge stood at the doorway, shoulder leaning against the jamb, arms loosely crossed against his chest. "I take it you like this room?"

"It's marvelous. You wanted a studio. This is the most perfect room for a studio I've ever seen." In fact, when the owner had first showed Lyssa this room, she felt a pang of envy. Any artist would love this room. The light, the space. The storage closets and shelves. Her own studio was a small catchall room in back of her house—"maid's room" would be the Realtor's term.

He pushed off the jamb, walked slowly to her, the Harrison Ford smile aimed at her. "Good. I needed an artist's professional opinion." Stopping in front of her, he cupped her chin with his palm and brought his mouth down for a tender kiss.

She leaned into him, her lips melting into his, soft, warm, clinging.

"I'll take it."

Lyssa's eyelashes fluttered up. She had been falling into the bottomless delight of his kiss. Any time, anywhere, whenever he kissed her, she responded with instant heat, instant craving.

She blinked a few times to orient herself back into real-estate mode, cleared her throat. "Great. Let's go back to the office and I'll draw up—"

A low rumble from deep in his chest grew to a chuckle. "Not so fast. I have some questions first."

"Okay, shoot."

"If you were buying, would you be comfortable living here?"

"Are you kidding?" She emitted an unladylike snort. "If it wasn't for the size of the mortgage payments, I'd snap up this place in a heartbeat. It has so much...*soul*. Texture. There are nooks and crannies to draw the eye. Closet space and built-ins galore. The gardens—let's just say, if I had a fulltime gardener, I'd be absolutely delighted to live here. I'd cut flowers every day and stick them all over the house."

"What about this room?"

Lyssa felt her eyes go all gooey, as though she was eyeing a particularly delectable chocolate torte. "Oh, yes. This room is an artist's dream. The light...it's lambent. And at night, there's the two strips of track lighting. It's just about perfect."

"Good. Now I have another question."

"Yes?"

"We've been dating for almost three months now. We've been to the Linc to root for the home team. We've watched the opera and the ballet. We've heard a few orchestras, hit all the museums in a hundred-mile radius. We've made the rounds of ethnic restaurants, even a gelato at Capogiro." He pulled her close to him, encircled her with his arms. "Does that qualify as a courtship?"

"I—uh—I guess so." Lyssa didn't dare say anything else.

"Would you say we have a modern relationship?"

Lyssa could feel her ears heating up. Yeah, it was modern. While they were careful not to be blatant about it—Evann only knew that he called her often at work—she'd spent many a night in his bed or he in hers, making love until she was sore in the most delicious places. She had no clue what her neighbors thought, if they peered out their windows checking to see whether or not his car would pull in the garage on a particular evening. When Michelle asked about Savidge in their weekly phone calls, she tried to keep it light and general. She certainly didn't want to flaunt their relationship when she fervently hoped Michelle wasn't promiscuous.

"Yeah, we do."

"So the next step would be to move in together, don't you think?"

At that, Lyssa's breath caught. Slowly she lifted her gaze to his. When she could find her voice, she said, "Here?"

"Yes, my sexy, beautiful, talented artist. Here. Could you live in this house? Paint in this room? Cook in that kitchen? No strings attached. Unless you want them. Really, it wouldn't be much different than what we're already doing, it's just that you'd be moving your clothes and art stuff here."

It seemed to Lyssa that he rushed the last sentence, as though to ride roughshod over any objection she might have.

He cleared his throat. "Of course, if you don't want to live here, maybe I'll have to move in with you. Because, if you'll remember, I just signed that contract of sale you negotiated, and I have to be out of that museum of mine within a month."

Lyssa bit back a smile. The self-assured, worldly, debonair Robert Savidge sounded, at that moment, as unsure as a sophomore asking his first date for a kiss.

"Let's go downstairs. I need to get something from my purse."

If he was disappointed at her lack of enthusiasm, he hid it well. Even though she'd surrendered her will and her trust to him the night Michelle all but forced them together, he'd allowed her to set the pace for their relationship. He'd never taken her for granted, never talked down to her, never ruled her with the iron hand her ex had. He treated her like an equal, and sometimes put her on a pedestal.

All this flitted through her head as she led him downstairs to the kitchen. She retrieved her purse, and, opening a zipper inside another zippered pocket, pulled out the precious item she'd carried with her since the day it was given to her.

And slipped it on her ring finger, left hand.

She turned to him, lifting her left hand with its platinum ring, to place her fingers gently on his arm. "When you gave me this ring, you said you wanted me to make a conscious decision."

His eyes glittered fiercely as his gaze followed her hand.

"This is my decision. I'm remembering the man who gave it to me. I don't want any other man. I want you. Only you. I'm not ready for marriage. My previous one still leaves a bad taste in my mouth. But I will say this. I don't want to live my life without you in it."

He brought her hand up to his lips and kissed each knuckle. "The only taste I want to leave in your mouth is — this." He dipped his head down and kissed her with all the fervor of a man who knew what he wanted and had just won it. His tongue plunged into her mouth, hot and demanding. She responded with an answering heat and demand, her tongue boldly stroking his, her body shaping itself to his hard muscles.

After a sizzling interval of their tongues dueling and thrusting, of their hands roaming over each other's bodies, Savidge murmured against her mouth, "I think we should christen this kitchen, don't you?"

"We can't. It wouldn't be right."

"Sure it would. You're a member of the Platinum Society. Your moral turpitude forces you to perform unthinkable, despicable acts while showing unsuspecting clients the kitchen of their dreams…"

Lyssa giggled.

He spun her around and positioned her with her elbows on the center island, then leaned over her and rubbed against her ass. "Feel that? It's your fault. I'm going to have to do something about that."

Another giggle escaped her. "Then it's a good thing I'm wearing a loose skirt."

"I think you planned this, woman," he growled into her ear just before he nipped it with his teeth.

She wiggled her ass into him. "Better make it fast. The owner's coming back at six. According to the clock on the wall, we have twenty minutes."

"It won't even take that long if you keep wiggling. I'm harder than these ceramic tiles."

With one quick swoop, he pulled the hem of her skirt up above her ass. And groaned. He'd just discovered another secret — she wasn't wearing panties.

A quick flick of his zipper and he was inside her from behind, his cock hard and hot in her cunt, thrusting savagely into her.

This was what she wanted. The man of her dreams, the home of her dreams, the fuck of her life, every time. Oh, she loved him. She wanted to admit it, almost did blurt it out as she felt him tense in a certain way that told her he was near to coming.

And maybe she would tell him. But not now, not when she was biting her lip to keep from screaming his name as he slammed her against the counter, not when she was coming, coming...

They exploded simultaneously, probably the quickest pop either of them had ever experienced.

All she could say later was, good thing it only took sixty seconds. Because at the instant of climax, she'd heard the garage door open, and a minute later Savidge had ducked into the powder room to clean up as she greeted the owner with the happy news of a sale.

Trademarks Acknowledgement

The author acknowledges the trademarked status and trademark owners of the following wordmarks mentioned in this work of fiction:

Aston Martin: Aston Martin Lagonda Limited

Bentley: Bentley Motors (1931) Limited Corporation

BMW: B 130, BMW Haus, Postfach

Dior: Christian Dior Couture, S.A.

Donna Karan: Gabrielle Studio, Inc.

Evian: Societe Anonyme Des Eauz Minerales D'Evian Corporation

FedEx: Federal Express Corporation

GQ: Advance Magazine Publishers Inc. Corporation

Guinness: Guinness PLC

Harrod's: Harrods Limited, London

Honda CR-V: Honda Giken Kogyo Kabushiki Kaisha (Honda Motor Co., Ltd.)

Manolo Blahnik: Blahnik; Manolo INDIVIDUAL

Mercedes-Benz: Daimler-Benz Aktiengesellschaft Corporation.

Mustang: Ford Motor Company

Patek Phillipe: Henri Stern Watch Agency, Inc.

Porsche Boxster: Dy. Ing. h. c. F. Porsche Aktiengesellschaft

Trademarks Acknowledgement
continued

Ritz Carlton: The Ritz-Carlton Hotel Company, L.L.C. LTD LIAB CO

Rolls Royce: Rolls-Royce Limited

Shalimar: Guerlein, Inc

Sprite: Coca-Cola Company, The

Tiffany: Tiffany & Company

Victoria's Secret: V Secret Catalogue, Inc.

7-Up: Seven-Up Company, The

About the author:

Cris Anson firmly believes that love is the greatest gift…to give or to receive. In her writing, she lives for the moment when her characters realize they love each other, usually after much antagonism and conflict. And when they express that love physically, Cris keeps a fire extinguisher near the keyboard in case of spontaneous combustion. Multi-published and twice EPPIE-nominated in romantic suspense under another name, she was usually asked to tone down her love scenes. For Ellora's Cave, she's happy to turn the flame as high as it will go—and then some.

Married for twenty years to her real-life hero, Cris enjoys slow dancing with him to the Big Band music of the Forties. She also plays the piano, nurtures a small garden at their home in eastern Pennsylvania, wishes she had time to bicycle more often, and is known to break out in song (yes, she can carry a tune) when the spirit moves her.

Cris welcomes mail from readers. You can write to her c/o Ellora's Cave Publishing at 1056 Home Avenue, Akron OH 44310-3502.

Why an electronic book?

We live in the Information Age—an exciting time in the history of human civilization in which technology rules supreme and continues to progress in leaps and bounds every minute of every hour of every day. For a multitude of reasons, more and more avid literary fans are opting to purchase e-books instead of paperbacks. The question to those not yet initiated to the world of electronic reading is simply: *why?*

1. *Price.* An electronic title at Ellora's Cave Publishing and Cerridwen Press runs anywhere from 40-75% less than the cover price of the <u>exact same title</u> in paperback format. Why? Cold mathematics. It is less expensive to publish an e-book than it is to publish a paperback, so the savings are passed along to the consumer.

2. *Space.* Running out of room to house your paperback books? That is one worry you will never have with electronic novels. For a low one-time cost, you can purchase a handheld computer designed specifically for e-reading purposes. Many e-readers are larger than the average handheld, giving you plenty of screen room. Better yet, hundreds of titles can be stored within your new library—a single microchip. (Please note that Ellora's Cave and Cerridwen Press does not endorse any specific brands. You can check our website at www.ellorascave.com or

www.cerridwenpress.com for customer recommendations we make available to new consumers.)

3. *Mobility.* Because your new library now consists of only a microchip, your entire cache of books can be taken with you wherever you go.

4. *Personal preferences are accounted for.* Are the words you are currently reading too small? Too large? Too...**ANNOYING**? Paperback books cannot be modified according to personal preferences, but e-books can.

5. *Instant gratification.* Is it the middle of the night and all the bookstores are closed? Are you tired of waiting days—sometimes weeks—for online and offline bookstores to ship the novels you bought? Ellora's Cave Publishing sells instantaneous downloads 24 hours a day, 7 days a week, 365 days a year. Our e-book delivery system is 100% automated, meaning your order is filled as soon as you pay for it.

Those are a few of the top reasons why electronic novels are displacing paperbacks for many an avid reader. As always, Ellora's Cave and Cerridwen Press welcomes your questions and comments. We invite you to email us at service@ellorascave.com, service@cerridwenpress.com or write to us directly at: 1056 Home Ave. Akron OH 44310-3502.

THE
ELLORA'8 CAVE
LIBRARY

Stay up to date with Ellora's Cave Titles
in Print with our Quarterly Catalog.

To recieve a catalog,
send an email with your name
and mailing address to:

CATALOG@ELLORASCAVE.COM
or send a letter or postcard
with your mailing address to:
Catalog Request
c/o Ellora's Cave Publishing, Inc.
1337 Commerce Drive #13
Stow, OH 44224

Lady *Jaided* Regular Features

Jaid's Tirade
Jaid Black's erotic romance novels sell throughout the world, and her publishing company Ellora's Cave is one of the largest and most successful e-book publishers in the world. What is less well known about Jaid Black, a.k.a. Tina Engler is her long record as a political activist. Whether she's discussing sex or politics (or both), expect to see her get up on her soapbox and do what she does best: offend the greedy, the holier-than-thous, and the apathetic! Don't miss out on her monthly column.

Devilish Dot's G-Spot
Married to the same man for 20 years, Dorothy Araiza still basks in a sex life to be envied. What Dot loves just as much as achieving the Big O is helping other women realize their full sexual potential. Dot gives talks and advice on everything from which sex toys to buy (or not to buy) to which positions give you the best climax.

On the Road with Lady K
Publisher, author, world traveler and Lady of Barrow, Kathryn Falk shares insider information on the most romantic places in the world.

Kandidly Kay
This Lois Lane cum Dave Barry is a domestic goddess by day and a hard-hitting sexual deviancy reporter by night. Adored for her stunning wit and knack for delivering one-liners, this Rodney Dangerfield of reporting will leave no stone unturned in her search for the bizarre truth.

A Model World
CJ Hollenbach returns to his roots. The blond heartthrob from Ohio has twice been seen in Playgirl magazine and countless other publications. He has appeared on several national TV shows including The Jerry Springer Show (God help him!) and has been interviewed for Entertainment Tonight, CNN and The Today Show. He has been involved in the romance industry for the past 12 years, appearing on dozens of romance novel covers and calendars. CJ's specialty is personal interviews, in which people have a tendency to tell him everything.

Hot Mama Cooks
Sex is her food, and food is her sex. Hot Mama gives aphrodisiac a whole new meaning. Join her every month for her latest sensual adventure -- with bonus recipe!

Empress on the Mount
Brash, outrageous, and undeniably irreverent, this advice columnist from down under will either leave you in stitches or recovering from hang-jaw as you gawk at her answers to reader questions on relationships and life.

Erotic Fiction from Ellora's Cave
The debut issue will feature part one of "Ferocious," a three-part erotic serial written especially for Lady Jaided by the popular Sherri L. King.

COMING TO A BOOKSTORE NEAR YOU!

ELLORA'S CAVE
2005
BEST SELLING AUTHORS TOUR

Lady Jaided magazine is devoted to exploring the sexuality and sensuality of women. While there are many similarities between the sexual experiences of men and women, there are just as many if not more differences. Our focus is on the female experience and on giving voice and credence to it. Lady Jaided will include everything from trends, politics, science and history to gossip, humor and celebrity interviews, but our focus will remain on female sexuality and sensuality.

A Sneak Peek at Upcoming Stories

Clan of the Cave Woman
Women's sexuality throughout history.

The Sarandon Syndrome
What's behind the attraction between older women and younger men.

The Last Taboo
Why some women – even feminists – have bondage fantasies

Girls' Eyes for Queer Guys
An in-depth look at the attraction between straight women and gay men

Available Spring 2005